# CRYSTALS AND DRAGONS

# NOTICE

This book is intended as a reference only, not as a medical manual. This book is not intended to be an exhaustive overview, but is designed to aid the reader in making informed decisions about health and wellness. As new information broadens our knowledge, change in programming and standards are required. All sources in this publication are believed to be reliable in their efforts to provide information that is complete and generally in accordance with the standards accepted at the time of publication.

The suggestions recommended in this publication are not intended as a substitute for any advise or instructions prescribed by a doctor. The advice contained herein should not be considered to be medical, legal or any other professional advice. All readers are advised to take full responsibility for their actions and understand their limits. The publisher and the author hereby disclaim any liability or loss in connection with the use of this book and advice herein.

**ETERNAL ICE**

For more of our products or information visit **eternal-ice.com**

# Dedication

*To Tom Sanford, Scott Sanford and Roger Sanford, my wonderful sons, thank you for all your love and support. You are all unique with amazing gifts. I am proud of the men you have become!*

*To all my friends, my extended family, I am grateful for all of you. Bless you for choosing to participate in my journey.*

*Thanks, Molly Rowland, for sharing your amazing gift of channeling and introducing me to the ascended masters.*

*Danielle Theodore, without you I don't know if this book would have ever been published. Thanks for all your hard work.*

*Mom, you accomplished so much in your life. It was time for you to fly free. Thanks for always having my back even when it was a challenge to believe in my journey.*

*Beyond anyone else in this lifetime, Bob, my love, my soul flame, you always believed in me, supported me and loved me. You taught me so much. I miss you.*

# CRYSTALS AND DRAGONS
## AN INTRODUCTION

*WHAT IS NEW AGE, ANYWAY?*

*"It's people taking conscious responsibility for their own lives, not blaming others for their problems.*
*It's people who deliberately decide to learn and grow.*
*It's people that don't have to be right, except for themselves.*
*It's people seeing problems as lessons, perhaps in a long series of lives and lessons.*
*It's people who believe we are what we think we are and can change ourselves by changing our thinking.*
*It's people that feel they can change the world by changing themselves, not by trying to change others.*
*It's people who search for strength from the universe by going inside themselves.*
*It's people that recognize love doesn't have to have conditions attached.*
*It's people loving and knowing themselves in order to better know and love others.*
*It's people who see others as not better than nor less than, but rather different than, themselves, yet part of the same whole.*
*It's people that choose their own path rather than follow dogma.*
*It's people honoring your right to your own path, not theirs.*
*It's people who realize that now is all we have, since yesterday is just a thought and so is tomorrow.*
*It's people interested in owning themselves rather than things.*
*It's people who see joy in life rather than pain, having experienced enough pain already.*
*It's people curious about extra sensory perception and all it implies.*
*It's people in all walks of life, from business persons to flower essence healers, psychologists to UFO investigators.*
*New Age is not a new religion with a hierarchy of priests and rituals, seeking converts, though some new agers choose some ritual.*
*New Age is not often about gloom and doom, though many are concerned about ecology, the economy and other forces that affect our world.*
*New Age is not a movement based on guilt, anger, fear or hurt; it is a journey toward the love that is God.*
*New Age is not allegiance to one master; it is learning from many masters in the quest for the oneness of God.*
*New Age could not become a cult because of what is said above.*
*New Age is not just humans doing, it is humans being."*

*- Anonymous*

**A**s I created this book, I didn't realize just how many feelings and emotions would arise. I admit there was a bit of fear there, also. Those things are ones I continue to deal with and it has created amazing healing within me. For those of you who are led to purchase and read this book, hopefully you will find wonderful new ways of using stones and crystals to better your life as well as the lives of others. The concepts you will find in these pages will perhaps amaze you, almost certainly cause you to expand your mind and hopefully trigger a remembrance of things as old as time. As you read, I encourage you to search the inner recesses of yourself, have fun with the ideas and always use your discernment, seeking your own special truth. The stories are true and things that I have experienced on my way to doing the crystal layouts and talking to others about what is important to them. The crystal information is primarily channeled through Molly Rowland from the Ascended Masters and the Brotherhood of Light. This is information you can rely on and that I have referred to over and over again. Some of that information has come through dreams, as it seems I am able to receive more readily through the dream state. All in all, this is the story of my life on the path to greater enlightenment and along the way I've created some interesting challenges for myself.

I have lived most of my life in Powell, Wyoming, a small town nestled in the northwestern part of the state called the Big Horn Basin. Clean, pretty and peaceful, it is surrounded by mountains often capped with snow, leaving just enough room for the farming and ranching so important to our economy. Very little serious crime exists and the people are friendly and outgoing, making it an ideal place to raise a family and develop lasting friendships. I was like most of the girls of my generation and area. Our one goal was to get married and have a family. It was rather expected of us. I fell in love very early in my life and married my sweetheart when I was a junior in high school. I finished my senior year in school two months after my first son was born and soon welcomed two more sons and a daughter. I raised my family, went through the anguish of losing my only daughter, cried when my marriage didn't survive the stress. The main thing I took away from my daughter's death was that wherever she was, it was a good and happy place. I was a single parent with very little money but we had a lot of love in our home. The tragedies didn't end there. My dad and my brother died in an accident together and my world fell apart. My emotions left me open for a very destructive and violent relationship. It seems the path I have chosen to experience this lifetime has been spent tying up loose ends and karmic ties. The choices I made weren't good ones but I was learning a lot about myself. There was a third marriage that taught me even more about myself. I delved into why I seemed to be drawing the same types of relationships and what I could do to change my path. I began to understand that I would have to heal myself before I could draw to me the relationship I desired.

One day I woke up and realized I was forty and once again in a very unhappy marriage. My children had grown up and were on their own and I was desperately seeking SOMETHING! The universe applauded, having thought, I am sure, that I would never ask. "When the student is ready..." My teacher was Liisa.

# TABLE OF CONTENTS

# DEFINITIONS

**MAGIK** - This spelling of the word magik differentiates between magical tricks and illusions and the truly ancient magik of long ago.

**CHAKRA** - Chakras are vortices of energy that relate to our energy fields and our energetic bodies. There are seven recognized with another opening in the thymus area. Each is a different color and vibration.

**KUNDALINI** - The kundalini is your life force energy. It is situated at the base of the spine. As your vibration rises, this energy awakens, moving the length of the spine, connecting you to your higher self.

**ASCENDED MASTER** - These are spiritual beings who, through experiences on this earth, have elevated their energy to the point where they have ascended. Many of them, such as Jesus, are well known and others remain anonymous.

**CRYSTAL** - The word crystal denotes different stones that have a crystalline form. While we associate a crystal as a Quartz crystal, many stones can form in different crystal shapes.

**CRYSTAL LAYOUT** - This refers to the practice of laying stones and crystals on the body for the purpose of aiding in the removal of blocks and other challenges from the body and energy field.

**REINCARNATION** - As we go through the process of beginning to remember who we truly are, we experience many lifetimes. This series of experiences brings you to a point of ascension. We refer to past lives but as you evolve, you will begin to understand that everything happens in the now.

**CRYSTAL ENERGY LEVEL** - On each page of the Stones and Crystals chapter, you will notice a small crystal. I have assigned an energy level to each stone pertaining to what I feel from it. You might feel something different but this gives you an idea of the energy of the stones.

# 1
# GETTING ACQUAINTED
# WITH MYSELF

*"We must cast off the heavy yoke of fear weighing down our soul and achieve greatness through honest self-reflection."*

*- Unknown*

Liisa was the wife of an acquaintance and had just arrived in Powell from the golden state of California. I think she was feeling a little lost, a newlywed plopped down in a remote place with few friends and fewer prospects. We hit it off right away and were soon visiting whenever we had the chance. I delighted in hearing about her life in California and the things in which she was involved. She actually had firsthand experience in automatic writing, classes on ESP and channeling plus a multitude of other things with which I was fascinated. We became fast friends, helping each other through the breakup of our marriages, working at the same job and exploring the myriad of subjects that interested us both. How excited we were! It was as if we had discovered things no one else had ever imagined. Every aspect of my life began to change.

One day Liisa called me, very excited and said, "Linda, I read in the paper that a meditation group is beginning. Would you be interested?" Would I! We got the paper out and looked and looked for the ad. Imagine our amazement when we couldn't find it anywhere! What was that all about? She was sure she had seen the ad but finally we just looked at each other and shrugged, acknowledging the mystery.

Just when the time was right, two years after the fact, there appeared an ad in the newspaper about a meditation group that was forming! Liisa and I had a good laugh over that and so began another chapter in our lives.

During this time, life went on as it does and I met my 'soul flame', Bob. He, like I, was searching. Bob, Liisa and I were like the three Musketeers. We went everywhere together. There was dancing and drinking, picnics and excursions, and, of course, our meditation group. That first group developed into another and still another as our ideas changed and we searched for other challenges. By this time, we knew there was more to this than the physical things associated with being psychic. We were beginning to delve into the spiritual path and were aware of others desiring to do the same. Bob, who was now my husband, and I organized another group, mostly beginners. We met at our home every week for a year, exploring everything we could find, then went our separate ways to seek what life had in store for us.

What a great period in my life! I was intensely interested in what I was learning, Bob and I both had great jobs and we were more and more in love, with each other, with ourselves and with life.

Then slowly, everything began to change. Surely that wasn't a nudge I felt! I was perfectly content. But yes, I have to admit I was being urged on to greater things. What does that look like?! I was soon to find out.

During our explorations, Liisa and I were lamenting the fact that we could find very few books on 'alternative thinking.' Those were found in a bookstore, a hundred miles away, tucked into a dark corner under an occult heading. We decided our area needed a good bookstore that would provide us with what we wanted. Are we good at manifesting?! The next day I opened the local paper to find an ad listing our local bookstore for sale! At the time, the store was quite small and carried a variety of books. 'Out on a Limb' by Shirley MacLaine was the only book close to what we were interested in. So, what do you do when something is dropped in your lap? You buy it! So long good paying job! Would Bob ever begin to understand that this was something I had to do? Would we manage on half the money we were bringing in until the store began to pay for itself? Bob did understand and now The Dragon and Unicorn Bookstore belonged to me, well, to the bank and me. I began to expand the inventory, adding metaphysical books, tarot cards and CRYSTALS. I was delirious! What fun for someone who has always had a love affair with books. I now had access to any book I wanted.

I loved that bookstore. There were children's books, religious texts, the self-help section and most everything else one would want to read. But my favorite section was the metaphysical items. I was learning a lot and felt everyone else would be as excited as I was. Color me naïve! After sharing my new-found excitement and hearing many negative reactions, I went from being extremely excited about what I was learning to hiding very quietly in the closet. I began to allow fear to rule my life. There was a man in our town who visited the bookstore on a regular basis. He kept close tabs on everything I was stocking in the store and one day asked me if I was one of those 'New Agers.' I muttered something unintelligible and went about my business. He then asked me to order him a book, which I proceeded to do. When the book came in, I was shocked to find it was all about how to make poisons, construct explosives and how to kill someone very quickly. I admit my imagination got the better of me and I was nearly sick with the fear. Before this time, I had no idea of how debilitating fear could be. When someone says they were paralyzed with fear, I can totally relate to that fear. It brought me to my knees, so to speak. The time came when I could no longer tolerate living that way and for three days and nights I wrestled with my demons and fears.  On the morning of the fourth day, I stepped into the shower and cried, "Enough!!"  I felt the mixture of tears and water running down my face and then the burden of my fear began to lift as if it were running down the drain. When I stepped from the shower, I felt as if I was many pounds lighter and ready to face what the universe had planned for me. One night I attended a program on channeling and looked up to find this man there. I was shocked because he was so against anything like that but even more impressed that he had the courage to ignore his fears. I knew deep down he would be at the bookstore the next morning so I prepared myself as well as I could. I was right! First thing the next morning, there he was. He sat down at my desk and we just looked at each other. He really was curious about me and what I was all about so I spoke from my truth. I told him I carried the things I did and wanted to learn more about so that I could help others and that I did that out of love. He looked at me for a moment and then said, "I'll bet you do." Then he walked out and never came back to the store. I did and still do see this man from time to time but the charge is gone and we have come to respect each other.  I bless him for playing his part as I learned a great deal. I came to realize later that if you are in a state of love, you won't experience fear. They are opposites and you won't feel them at the same time. It's impossible. If you find yourself in a constant state of fear, begin to affirm the love. "I choose love. I am love." If you find you can't even do that, just say the word love over and over. You will find yourself in an amazing cocoon of loving energy.

Years before, when I was visiting Virginia, a friend asked me if I would like to go with her to an astrology class. I was up for that so we went to the meeting. The very first thing we were told we were going to do was a guided meditation. Now, I have always resisted that type of meditation as it seemed they were all the same. Sure enough, we were directed to walk down a forest path, meet a being who had a gift for us and a message. Oh, well, when in Rome, do as the Romans do. As I was meditating, I was greeted by a spirit guide who gifted me with the most amazing Emerald crystal. He told me it was for my healing. It has come in handy more than once. There were times of intense fear when I was told by spirit to go into my Emerald. There was always love and safety in that energy. Of course, all of these things were happening on a spiritual, energetic level. These things were beginning to emerge as I allowed myself to open to greater clarity and acceptance. The lessons on this earth might seem harsh but if we allow, the most wonderful things come to us. Years later, I was looking through an art catalog and came across a picture that was exactly like the being I saw! I yelled to my husband, "It's him, it's him" and promptly purchased the print. It has a place of honor in my healing center. So much for guided meditation!

Evidently, I felt I had to test myself one more time. You think you've mastered your fear? Here's a pop quiz!  Everything came to a head when I received a long-distance phone call from a woman who introduced herself as Molly Rowland, card reader and astrologer, who was touring throughout the Northwest. She wished to know if she could work at my store for a week or so. I thought that was a wonderful idea and told her to make her plans. Molly placed a small ad in the local newspaper announcing her visit and everything was set.

She arrived the day before she was to begin and after being settled in our guest room, we began to get acquainted. We could never have guessed how this inauspicious beginning would affect others and us for years to come.

When Molly and I arrived at the store the next morning, I was handed an innocent looking envelope. I opened it to find a copy of Molly's ad from the paper and a petition signed by about fifty people from two of the churches in town stating that if I didn't cancel Molly's visit, they would no longer frequent my business. The letter also said that I was corrupting the kids in our fine town, promoting Satanism and generally doing things with which they didn't agree. They had decided we didn't need people like Molly in our town. I was really shocked and felt like I had been punched in the stomach. What was I going to do? Should I give in to them? There was really no question about that. I knew I wouldn't cancel Molly's visit.

As I was digesting all this, a man from the newspaper walked in to see about some advertising. I practically shoved the letter in his face and said, "See what I got?!" He read the letter and then asked me if I wanted to follow up on it. (A reporter knows a good thing when he sees it!) Pushing down panic, I said yes! He left, promising to send a reporter to see us. A short time later, the reporter did arrive. He interviewed Molly and me and took pictures. Now there was nothing to do but wait for the next day's paper and tell my mother that we were going to be in it. My mom was very fearful for me and didn't think I should have a confrontation with the churches. I hadn't realized that my grandmother was a member of one of the protesting churches. Mom shared that grandma cried about the situation and wanted to know what I was doing. I assured them both as best I could and hoped they would understand I had to do this to finally stand for who I am.

Oh, no! Oh, yes! We hit the front page! "Churches Protest Astrologer" read the headline under our picture, a picture showing the tarot cards on the table. Very symbolic! I guess this means I'm out of the closet big time! How will people react? What will they think? Why am I so concerned about that anyway? This is an ongoing concern for me and invades most areas of my life. I've always, for as long as I can remember, done everything I knew to get people to love me. If I said this or did that, I might be rejected. If I showered people with gifts or bought lunch every time, I would really be appreciated. This confrontation in my life began a healing that is a work in progress. I'm learning to remember who I AM and that I don't have to buy love. I am only required to acknowledge that the love is within me. And that is truly where it has to start and end.

I learned something that day. My truth is the safest place to be. I had stood up for what I believed, despite the desire to run, and everything I heard was an affirmation. There were no negative comments in the store at all. The publicity was invaluable and Molly was booked solid and even extended her stay! People would come in to the store and say, "We didn't know you had this stuff in here. Keep up the good work! Don't let them get to you!" It was quite a coming out party!

There were many letters to the editor in the next few weeks, both pro and con. I didn't enter into that conflict because I believe everyone is entitled to his or her beliefs. I simply desire the same consideration. A wonderful aftermath of this episode is that since I didn't give in to these people, they left me alone. And I have never felt that kind of fear again.

# 2

# EXPLORING A CRYSTAL PATH

*I am strong because I have experienced.*

During this time, my interest in crystals was growing and I was reading everything I could get my hands on about using the crystals. I was especially interested in the healing aspects. You guessed it! I was being nudged in yet another direction. And the teacher appeared in the form of Bernie.

One day, a dear friend called to tell me that a class on crystal healing was beginning in Billings, Montana, which is about a hundred miles north of Powell. It was the middle of the winter when Old Man Winter gets in a rage and lets the world hear about it. The roads are sometimes fearful avenues of ice and snow and the howling wind encloses you in a cocoon of white. Still, the pull of the class drew me and I knew I had to do this. Once a week, I drove the two-hundred-mile round trip to learn about these wonderful tools I had discovered. Our classes were a mixture of theory and hands-on techniques. Learn by doing. And I learned a lot.

The night came when Bernie demonstrated a crystal layout. The class gathered around and she began. I was quite simply enthralled and lost in the wonder of it all. The one thing I remember most clearly was the desire to tell her to step aside because I knew how to do this! I have been doing this from the beginning of time! Consciously, I didn't know much about the crystals or even how to identify them. I recognized Clear Quartz, Amethyst and Rose Quartz but little else. But, even with that being the case, I felt the crystals as a part of me. I was remembering anew the magik of the work.

I will always be grateful to Bernie for the love and understanding of crystals and stones she passed on to me. I consider her a special friend. (Bernie has since crossed over and I trust she is still enjoying her love of healing and especially the crystals!)

After twelve weeks, the classes concluded and I was certified to do crystal healing! I continued to read every crystal book that was published but was somewhat disturbed by the many limitations I discovered in them. I knew at a soul level there was more and so I used what I could and continued my search.

Molly returned that summer, bringing with her a friend named Pat. They came to work for a week and stayed for nearly a year! What a time that was! Molly was learning to trans-channel and was brought to a place of safety to do that. Pat helped me out in the bookstore and in our spare time we learned and processed what we had learned and learned some more. Often, we yelled or laughed or cried. Just try putting three independent females in one house, on the same path to be sure, but with definite ideas and see what happens! God bless my husband who remained centered and at ease which kept the boat from rocking too much. That was a mostly quiet summer for him, as he couldn't get a word in edgewise, but he learned too.

Molly has the very special gift of channeling the Ascended Masters and the Brotherhood of Light, not just one of them, a lot of them. We got acquainted with Lord St. Germain, Lord Hilarion, Lord Michael, Lord Lanto and more. Their information was wonderful but the unconditional love and understanding were what we hungered for. No matter what we did or said, there was no judgment, only sharing and love. 'Tears are the fountain of youth.' And we cried. 'Be in joy.' And we laughed. 'Remember.' And we did our best. (I thought I was there. I thought I had done that.) 'You think too much. There is no 'there', only a plateau before the next upward spiral.' The foundation of our work on the path was being laid.

I made decisions that spring. The bookstore had served its purpose and the time had come to move on. I was and am a crystal healer and I had a lot to offer people. I needed to be free to do my work.

I closed the bookstore and as I packed up the last book and swept out the store one final time, I wondered what I would be led to do. I knew I wanted to work with crystals but how does one go about that? Our area was not exactly open to this idea of mine. Not to worry! As I embarked on my new adventure, the Masters gave me information on the stones and crystals and encouraged me to remember those things I had forgotten. I felt as if I had leaped empty-handed into the void and was learning to fly. There was no going back.

The doors started to open. Two weeks had passed and the phone rang. In the way of these things, the woman on the other end was looking for Molly, who had moved on. When we talked a bit and she found out I had crystals and books, she asked me to come to Cheyenne, Wyoming to work at a psychic fair she was arranging. I was thrilled. This would be a new experience for me and would also provide a way for me to meet other like-minded people.

My first experience with a psychic fair was mostly positive. I met many wonderful people, sold crystals and books and had a lot of fun. It was also a lot of hard work, carrying boxes of merchandise up two flights of stairs, setting everything up and then reversing the process at the end of the day. There were other inconveniences such as little or no parking, even to load and unload. We also had people come in to protest what we were doing which was really nothing new to me but it brought home to me that this path we followed was going to have some potholes! And I could hardly wait for more!

The next time I was called, I decided to do energy balancing as well as selling the books and crystals. I set up in a room that gave me privacy and waited, somewhat anxiously, to see what would happen. This was, after all, another step on the path. What if no one was interested? What would I do? Not to worry! I was overwhelmed by the response. I was busy all day and a line actually formed! I was being accepted! I felt relief but exhilaration, too. I knew I was following my calling and that people were in need of what I had to share.

I went on to do other fairs in Cheyenne and then, (surprise!) I decided I would like to try something more challenging. The workshops were being created.

I have a friend in Sheridan, Wyoming, who I knew was interested in all the wonderful things I was pursuing. One day I gave Monna a call and asked if she would arrange a workshop on crystal healing for me. I would also do private appointments. She agreed enthusiastically and once more I was on my way. The arrangements were made and I hung up.

As the time approached, I made ready to go. Another dear friend of mine, Pat Kent, was going with me to help with setting up and anything else that might arise. We left on Friday for the two-hour drive to Sheridan. Our route was over the Big Horn Mountains, beautiful and rugged. It was a truly delightful trip, clear and warm with wildflowers a riot of color against the evergreens and grass. Now and then, we caught a glimpse of soft brown, a deer nibbling the tender grass of spring or stopping to watch the machine that invaded her territory. The mood was set for a wonderful and fulfilling weekend.

We arrived at the home of Johanna where we would be staying and doing the workshop. She is a gifted massage therapist and a lovely person. The crystals were unloaded and set up and I was ready for this new adventure that remains a source of joy, even now.

It is a challenge to describe the feelings I have for this, my life work. I have the distinct pleasure of meeting and interacting with all kinds of people and maybe making a difference in their lives. I experience the joy of working with God energy, feeling what can't be put into words. And, I learn and grow and heal myself as I work with others.

This particular weekend held a grand surprise for me that made me realize some of what I would be dealing with in the future. Even now it sounds very bizarre to me. Several women had scheduled private sessions with me. These consist of laying stones on the body and moving the energy in such a way to remove blocks from the different energy levels. There are always a variety of responses to the sessions but one stands out in my mind like it happened yesterday. Everything was progressing normally with the layout as we recognized and dealt with some minor emotional things. Suddenly, my client became extremely agitated. She said something was "munching" in her ear! Oookay. I calmed her down (a little) and proceeded to try to figure out what was happening and what I was going to do about it. Knowing that Malachite was a 'drawing' stone, I placed a piece beside her ear and directed energy into the other ear. Imagine my surprise and disbelief when I 'saw' three small figures dive out of the ear and into the Malachite. My sigh of relief was short lived, however, when the woman practically screeched that it was still eating on her. As a friend of mine says, if it wasn't for the honor of the thing, I'd just as soon have been in Philadelphia! Finally, using a Malachite wand, I was able to draw out a nasty bit of psychic energy that was determined to stick around. Incredibly, this 'gargoyle' appeared to be about a foot tall and angry. He was quick as lightning and jumped here and there in the aura, hanging on for dear life. By this time, my client had a thick, protective blanket of energy around her but was still in a panic, thinking the entity, which she saw as all mouth and teeth, would enter her again. I finally took my laser crystal and cut the energy from the aura. I persuaded the manifestation to go to the light surrounded with love. (As I got more experience, I found other ways of dealing with that kind of energy such as putting it into the violet flame where it could be transmuted into a loving energy. When something is cut off from the fear that it feeds upon, it becomes weaker and weaker.) I calmed my client and removed the stones and crystals, some of which felt sticky from the negative energy. We cleansed the crystals, smudged the house and sat down to ponder what had transpired. Wow, was I going to have a talk with the Masters!

I learned several things from this session. Primarily, I recognized that in our fear, we manifest some mighty unsavory things for ourselves. In this particular case, the 'seed' of the manifestation had been carried through many lifetimes, arising from an ancient Chinese period when she had tremendous power and greatly misused it. Fearing she would again abuse her power, she created this 'seed' as a reminder. As each lifetime passed without resolving the fear, it became a living thing that fed constantly--on fear! By the time I saw it, it was incredibly powerful. I also learned that I was loved and protected and that I could call on the Masters or a Higher Source at any time. This sounds very basic but sometimes we get so caught up in what we're doing, we don't stop to ask for help. 'Ask and ye shall receive.' I remember thinking that if I could handle this thing, I could handle anything! Perhaps that was the greatest lesson. I was beginning to realize that I could make a difference--with a lot of help from my 'friends'! What a joyous feeling that is. As the weekend wound down, I was ecstatic. This was what I wanted to do more than anything.

# 3

# A NEW UNDERSTANDING

*"A healer reminds another that they themselves are the healer. He gives the gift of remembering to the cellular structure, the soul pattern, the memory banks. The spirit informs the wholeness. You cannot force the wholeness. Some you can't heal. Some will not give their permission."*

*- Jesus*

**A**t this point, I was learning a lot about feeling the energy of the crystals and discerning which ones of them would best be used for a particular client. As I had greater access to the Masters, they would give me the layouts ahead of time and I would follow what I was given. As I got more experience, I began to hear and sense what stones would be used for a particular client. As time sped up, this was preferable to getting the layouts a day or two ahead as everything was happening now. The layouts are beautiful and it feels as if the body is the blank canvas waiting to receive infinite patterns of crystals and colors. No two layouts are the same and the reactions are as varied as those who come to me for help. Some clients cry, some laugh, some sneeze and some leave their body entirely. There are those who move deeply within themselves in their healing and there are those who will go in a short way and stop. The energy of those people feels hard and sometimes they won't allow you to help them at all.

It is so important for everyone to understand that I cannot heal them nor can you heal someone else. We can facilitate that healing but the client has to be willing to allow the healing. Only they can heal themselves. The next thing everyone should understand is that all of us carry the seeds of all diseases within us at all times yet you only express dis-ease of a certain form when you have opened yourself to that through a certain viewpoint. For example, if you hate someone, that opens the body to diabetes, heart disease, hardening of the arteries and liver malfunction. Hatred affects all aspects of the body. It won't hurt the person you hate but most definitely it will be reflected within you.

Our emotions are the basis for all dis-ease in the body. If we deal with our emotions as we experience them, before they become physical, we heal much more easily. Pay attention to some of the old adages and what they say to us. How many people who suffer from stiff necks have a 'stiff-necked attitude'? How many rigid beings are locked in the embrace of arthritis? How many are sick and tired? How many do you know that allow themselves to be eaten up with their emotions and manifest cancers, ulcers? "I can't stomach that." "I am pissed off." Kidney disease. Bile is associated with the liver and we store our anger there or deposit it in gallstones. We are very creative when we require looking at something and have our heads stuck in the sand.

One young woman I worked with was a perfect example of those adages. She had psoriasis all over her body. It was so severe, cracked and bleeding, that I was reluctant to place the crystals on her. She also suffered from rheumatoid arthritis which I understand occurs regularly with psoriasis. We began to talk as I moved the energy over her body. Her relationship with her family was terrible. She was on the verge of a divorce and her children had no respect for her. If anything, her relationship with her mother was worse. I told her she needed to start dealing with her mother if she wanted to start healing. She said, and I quote, "Dealing with my mother makes me want to crawl out of my skin!" She had done a good job of it. I talked to her a few days later and she related to me that she had walked all the way to her vehicle before she noticed she had no pain. The healing had begun.

I have mentioned before the crystal laser. I always knew I had to have one and one day entered a metaphysical gift store that had crystals. There was a laser there that really called to me. I couldn't put it down. It was very powerful and I felt it would be a great addition to my healing crystals. It went home with me and I have it even now. I didn't know I feared the energy until it languished in my crystal box for over two years. I would pick it up and feel the energy but would never use it in my healing work. I guess I didn't feel I could handle that much energy and power. So many times, we bring memories with us lifetime after lifetime. If we have misused the energy or had unfortunate experiences with something, we become unwilling to deal with it again. I do know that this particular laser was one that was mine in Atlantis. It had a gold coil around the tip to amplify the energy. I was a healer in those times and may have had an unpleasant experience with it. Gradually, I got to the point of using it. It is a great instrument for use in difficult circumstances.

There came an opportunity to begin using the laser. A client came to me and I got the impression that she had a very thick wall around her heart chakra. As I was contemplating the situation, the Masters 'told' me to get my laser to begin to break up the wall. I'm sure I said something like "Are you crazy?? That is too strong for the heart area." As if the Masters don't know what they're doing! Finally, I got the laser and began to create chinks in that wall. Hey, the world didn't end and I didn't cause harm to anyone! And the wall started to crumble. Sometimes, we find unique ways to protect ourselves from fear, pain and heartbreak. This chakra is mostly about love and the challenges we have surrounding that emotion.

Lasers are a delicate formation of Quartz, short or long, but generally slender. They are used for cutting away inappropriate energies from the energy field and even the body. Many of you have heard of psychic surgery and may even have seen documentaries of the Philippine healers who reach into the body to remove tumors and other things from their clients. My laser works in much the same way but without any blood. It is an energetic cutting away of things that no longer serve.

# 4

# CHANGING PERSPECTIVE

*Beloved body! I am in love with you as you are. I forgive the pain I have labeled upon you and upon myself because I was not pleased. I forgive the possessiveness of this barrier of flesh and I give us permission to be in joy and beauty and comfort appropriate unto my highest good.*

**I**n our culture, most of us don't want to cry. We perceive it as a weakness, **particularly men.** Crying is a valuable tool we can use to deal with our emotions. The Masters tell us that tears are the fountain of youth. I found I spent a lot of time with clients telling them to set aside some time to cry, to give themselves permission to cry. For many, this was a new concept.

One day in Virginia, a woman came to me for healing work and, half defiantly, said she hadn't cried for three years. Having a good connection with the Masters, I heard a voice telling me to tell the woman to get and peel an onion. When the tears started, she was to let herself go and cry. I was pretty amazed. I would never have thought of that myself. As with many people, I sometimes doubt that I see and hear the things I do. I laugh and tell people I am a doubting Thomas. When I am in the greatest doubt is the time I hear something like in the episode with the onion that I know isn't something I made up. I am grateful for those things.

Working with the Masters has been such a blessing and a marvelous opportunity to learn and remember. If I push myself too hard and need reminding, one of the Masters is there. I'm reminded of one trip to the east coast where I spent nearly a month doing my healing work. Sometimes I would do three or four layouts a day to accommodate those who wanted a personal healing session. As I was preparing to do the fourth session one day, I looked up and standing across from me was St. Germain. He looked at me and said, "My, we're busy, aren't we?" I laughed because I knew exactly what he was saying to me. Later he gave me something to ponder. He told me that we are crystalline structures and asked me if I would drive seventy miles an hour down the interstate and throw one of my beautiful crystals out of the car window to see if it would break or not. Then he asked me why I would push myself to the breaking point as I was crystalline, too. The comparison really hit home because at the time I took second place to everything else. And I wouldn't do that to one of my stones! In addition to the loving reminders, we also have a lot of fun with the masters. They all have a great sense of humor. The Archangel Michael does what we call a 'ha-ha' mantra. He will start to laugh slowly, ha…ha…ha and then more rapidly. Soon, everyone has joined in and all are laughing. One day I was working with a young woman and strongly sensed the energy of Lord Michael. I asked her if she worked with him or was familiar with his energy. She wasn't so I told her she would love the energy and how much fun it was to work with him. This big booming voice (at least it seemed so to me) said, "How nice of you to say so!" Again, I laughed because these things are so unexpected and welcome.

I have had the opportunity to see how our emotions, and how we deal with them, greatly affect our lives. Do we do battle with our diseases and put our energy there? Do we do what we can and then focus on having a whole and healthy body? Are we strong enough to change our lives so we can change the outcome of our manifestations? Or did we make a soul agreement to experience a particular situation and have to see it through? Keep in mind that what has been created can be uncreated.

I drew two women to me who were mirror images of one another except in attitude. Both had had thyroid cancer with the thyroid gland being removed. Both had had breast cancer with one losing the left breast and the other losing the right breast. Both had submitted to radiation treatment. One was a medical doctor and the other a housewife. The doctor had become an MD to discover why she had gotten thyroid cancer. Her days were spent looking for cancer. She tested herself each day, never sure what she would find. She wasn't well when she came to me but she was sure she was going to show everyone and manifest a new breast. She worked with a group of healers who encouraged her to do this. This was a very karmic tie and she had lost her life many times to this same group who focused on what they could do and not how they could help her heal. Once again, she chose to work with them and the lesson went unlearned. So ultimately, she drew the cancer to her again. Two weeks after I saw her, she succumbed to the cancer. She had not been strong enough to make the drastic change in her life that would have helped her heal. She didn't realize that she had the power to do that.

The housewife had a completely different way of looking at things. She had made up her mind that she was going to lead a healthy and happy life after doing what she could about the cancer. When last I heard, she was still alive and well.

Both these women had undergone radiation treatment. Having seen psychically what radiation does to the body, I would personally opt to try something less damaging to my body. Radiation burns the body and it burns the energy body. A psychic surgeon can go into the aura and literally cut away dead 'meat' that looks like raw hamburger that has spoiled. Anyone who has experienced this treatment needs a lot of loving healing. This is such a personal decision and no one knows what they would do until faced with the choice. I honor these two women and all others who have to make that choice.

In the beginning stages of my healing work, I came across many people who really didn't understand that those of us involved in the spiritual work have challenges the same as everyone else. They tend to think we should be perfect and can't understand when we demonstrate our lack of perfection. I've been heavy most of my life and called many different names, none of them particularly nice. Children can be cruel but so can adults. One woman I recall meeting in Virginia was visiting at the home where I was staying to work. We were discussing the crystals and the way I worked with them. She turned and looked at me and said, "If you are a healer, why are you so fat?" I was caught off-guard and don't remember precisely what I said to her but I hope I got across to her that we all have challenges. I, too, put unrealistic expectations on those of us who were healers but created dis-ease in the body. Why, if we understood the how and why of healing, did we manifest these things and sometimes die from them? With all our tools, why weren't we healing ourselves? The answers to these questions are varied and deep. I don't pretend to understand the nuances of each person's creation. Do we feel unworthy of healing? Do we focus on the disease and not being healthy? Do we live in fear of the dis-ease? What does the dis-ease call attention to? This is why each person has to take responsibility for their own healing because the answers to the questions are unique to each individual. I also came to understand that a master never takes anything personally. Easier said than done!

# 5

# A SHARP STICK

*"I am not bound to win, but I am bound to be true. I am not bound to succeed. But I am bound to live up to the light I have."*

*- Abraham Lincoln*

**Many times, people will carry emotional manifestations over from a previous lifetime.** These things get stuck in the auras and cells and can cause discomfort in the present life. In particular, if a person has died in a violent way, he/she will carry that memory forward and it will manifest as a phobia or pain, seemingly having no known cause. I have become aware of daggers and swords sticking out of the backs of clients. Other times, there are infections and other apparent injuries. One of the beginning layouts I did was on a young woman in Virginia. My friend Doris had set up a workshop for me and at the end of the first day I was to do a private layout on a friend of hers. Molly was in the area and had decided to go have a bite to eat while I was busy. As I went through the process of scanning the body, I became aware of a large sword sticking up out of her back. She wasn't aware of anything there but I could definitely see it. These things are ideally removed when discovered so I set about doing that. This was a BIG sword and it was a comical situation attempting to remove something only I could see and wondering how I was going to do that when it was taller than I was! Doris was sitting in on this session and must have thought I was crazy. All she could see was air! About this time, Molly walked into the room through the door at the back and exclaimed, "Wow, would you look at the size of that sword!" I was gratified for the confirmation but to this day I know Doris thinks we set it up! Anyway, Molly helped me remove the sword and I proceeded to repair the injury to the aura. This client never did have a clue what that was all about but at least that was one less thing she had to deal with in this life.

My friend Doris, now known as Annalaiya, had many layouts with me. One time in particular stands out. We were dealing with some highly emotional issues concerning family and set about cutting the cords that connect us with other people. I asked if there was someone she would like to cut the emotional cords to and she indicated her sister. As soon as she said that, she yelled, "My eye, oh, my eye!" I asked her what had happened and she said it felt like someone poked her in the eye. I joked with her about it hurting like a poke in the eye with a sharp stick but it really wasn't funny and we ended the session soon after. When she got off of the table, her eye had turned blood red and was very painful. As we talked about the emotional connection to her sister, it turned out that in another lifetime she and her sister were knights who were jousting. She was very good at this and very arrogant so she decided to leave the visor up that covered her eyes. She died that day with a lance through her eye. In this lifetime, she and her sister had an argument as children and Annalaiya pushed her sister into a table with a sharp corner and it knocked her sister's eye off center. She never did recover an alignment of that eye. So many of these things, if explored, can give you insight into your relationships as well as dis-eases. From time to time, Annalaiya still has some pain in the eye but now she knows she requires dealing with this issue on an ever-deeper level. She has made peace with the situation and has let go of the guilt about her sister.

A lot of people find they aren't comfortable in this life and are not so sure they want to remain. This causes them in many cases to schism themselves, with parts of themselves going to different places and dimensions. Now we are becoming aware of those pieces of ourselves and the importance of bringing them back to us so that we might be whole again.

One young man I worked with experienced narcolepsy on a regular basis. This dis-ease causes one to fall asleep at inappropriate times and places. As he lay on the massage table I turned to look at him and saw, instead of one face, two. One was looking down and the other, up. I got the sense that his war with himself about staying in this life or leaving with the space brothers he was connected to, had effectively torn him in two. As we began to talk about this conflict, he came to see that in order to heal in this lifetime he would need to be fully present. He had agreed to experience this life and the lessons to be learned but so desired to go back to what he considered home. Sometimes the choices aren't easy ones.

"My name is Featherwoman," the woman I knew as Pat said as she sat up after a layout. I was a little surprised as she had never voiced an interest in changing her name as had some of my friends. Pat had become aware of Native American guides around her and lifetimes spent as a native. The culture drew her and culminated in an energy shift that married both this life and others. We all call her Feather, it's who she is. That is an example of how a part of ourselves can be brought back to make a whole. While not totally a split-off part of oneself, those lifetimes we experience are the sum total of who we are now. She succeeded in integrating that culture and this and became Featherwoman.

As you can see, the layouts accomplish many different things. Primary among them is an awareness of who we are and what we are about. As we become aware and deal with the attendant emotions, we begin our healing journey in earnest.

# 6

# CRYSTALS 101

*There is a difference between pushing for expansion and pushing to see
if the body will come apart or not. Pushing yourself in these times of
great upward spiral is like digging a ditch after major surgery.*

Once you have made the choice to explore the vast arena of stones, crystals and crystal healing, there are basic things to learn about how to care for these perfect bits of energy. These recommendations are also made to protect yourself and others. Once you begin to do these things on a regular basis, they will become second nature.

## CHOOSING YOUR CRYSTALS

"How do I know which crystal is mine?" I have heard those words many, many times. As I had crystals in the bookstore, I knew I had better learn this basic step so that I could help others pick what would work best for them. This was before crystal healing was even on my radar. I read everything I could get my hands on about the crystals. When I recognized the energy in each stone, I began to tune in to the vibrations that emanated from them. I could hold my left hand over several stones, one at a time, and feel the one that connected to me. Energy usually enters the left hand and leaves through the right. It is a cycle. Once in a while, I meet someone who is the opposite of that. The first thing I would have people do would be to choose a few of the stones they were attracted to and lay them out in a row. Then I would have them pass their hand over the stones one by one to see if one felt warmer or cooler or maybe had a tingle there. The left hand is primarily used for this as in the majority of people the energy comes into the left side and leaves through the right side completing the cycle. One woman I recall had the stones laid out and was attempting to choose which one spoke to her. She practically wailed that there was one crystal she kept coming back to but it was the ugliest one there! She wanted something very beautiful but the one that called her had the energy she required. She did purchase the stone and I trust she grew to love it as she bonded with the energy. A crystal doesn't have to look a particular way to work powerfully. In my practice, I use both rough and tumbled stones and stones that have been shaped into wands and points and made into elixirs. Some of the most powerful crystals are some of the least attractive but if you close your eyes and feel them, the energy is intense. Some people gravitate to the natural or unpolished stones more but the energy is going to work the same. St. Germain related to me that when a stone is polished or tumbled, it experiences the same effect that we would get if we took a fine grade of sandpaper and ran it over our skin. There is no lasting harm done. Another way to decide on that particular crystal or stone is to have someone muscle test you. This is a form of kinesiology. One would hold the crystal to the solar plexus, put the other arm out and have the other person ask silently if the stone was a match for the person then push down on the arm. If the arm stays strong, the answer is yes. If the arm goes down, it is time to look for something else. This is a great way of deciding things as your body won't lie. For those with an understanding of pendulums and the detachment to get a true result, this is another great method of determining your special tool. It is important to be detached and not expect a positive or negative response just because you like it or you don't. Each person will develop their own unique way of choosing and using these treasures from the earth. However you choose to do it, you're sure to find a crystal that vibrates to your energy.

## CLEANSING AND RECHARGING YOUR CRYSTALS

Once you have chosen a stone, it needs to be cleansed and charged. In nearly every book you pick up, you will be told to use salt or salt water to cleanse your stone and then set it in the sun to charge the energy. This has been an effective way to do this but it takes time and is sometimes harsh on the crystals. Keep in mind that the sun will begin to fade the colors of some crystals if you leave them there a long period of time. Amethyst and Rose Quartz are two of the most commonly affected. As I traveled across the country doing my healing work, I required a way of cleansing and recharging the crystals and stones quickly as sometimes I did three or four layouts in a day and used some of the same crystals and stones in each. In a layout the stones take on energy, both positive and negative, and they require to be cleansed after each use. I'll admit I wasn't very concerned about cleansing them immediately after use until the Masters reminded me that they continued to throw off that energy until cleansed. And, some of that energy was really negative!

The Masters gave me a kinder and gentler way of doing that and it was fast! I was told to make a solution of pyrite particles and pure water in a container large enough to handle the size of crystals most often used. I use a large plastic tub such as peanut butter or margarine comes in, one with a lid. Put a bag of pyrite into the container and rinse several times as this is an iron ore and has some residue in it. Then add distilled, filtered or pure well water to the container and cover. Let it sit overnight to charge the water. The pyrite stays in the water through many uses. When you feel the energy in the water has dissipated, put the used pyrite back on the earth and use new pyrite. Also, after a month or two, you might notice that the water has a form of algae floating in it. When that happens, just dump the water off of the pyrite, wash the pyrite and add fresh water. When you wish to cleanse a crystal, hold it under tepid water from the faucet to remove most of the negative energy and then swish it back and forth in the pyrite solution until the stone feels clear. Dry it and it is ready to use once more. (Do not let a stone sit in the solution as it might harm it!) Some would ask why we can sit in Epsom salt and water and it doesn't harm us but should not be used with the stones. Even though we are a crystalline structure, we have a barrier of flesh that protects that crystalline form. Crystals and stones do not have that protection and can become scratched or etched in the use of salt. Using pyrite is quick and efficient. I was recently asked if I recommended burying a crystal in the ground as a way of cleansing. If I had a stone that was very contaminated, that might be a method I would try but the pyrite solution works just as well. If you do bury it, be sure to mark the spot! Crystals also love the elements. Try placing your stones in the moonlight or the rain and tap into how the energy is reacting. It might surprise you. If you have only a few stones, this would work for you, but when you have as many as I work with, simpler is better! With a little experimentation, you will find a method that works for you and your beautiful stones.

## PROTECTION

When I was starting to get involved in the energy of the crystal healing, from what I read, protecting yourself with white light got the job done. I was diligent about doing that before every layout. One day I was doing a healing session that was quite intense but we accomplished it. Later, I became very uncomfortable, itching and hurting. I looked at myself and I had manifested hives starting at my hip and ending at my ankle. That really caught my attention! As I talked to spirit, I began to see that I was like an emotional sponge and was taking on what others were throwing off in the healing sessions. The white light was strong but required additional energy due to the more and more intense layouts. I was given an amazing way to do that. It works very well and I never have to worry about 'energy vampires' or negative energy and psychic attacks. You really should be vigilant about protecting yourself every day and each night, too. We travel in our dream state and it would be wise to protect yourself. If you find yourself in a particularly negative energy, it helps to reinforce your protection.

*Following is what I was given to protect myself. You can repeat the words verbatim or say it your way but be sure to keep the basics.*

*The innermost level is the white light followed by the violet in the center and the deep blue on the outside. Be sure to envision this energy surrounding your entire body as well as under your feet and over you head. It is like a cocoon of protection.*

*I call on the white Christ light for love and protection. Focus on making this as real as you can.*

*I call on the violet flame of Lord St. Germain for love and protection through transmutation.*

*I call on the midnight blue of the Archangel Michael for love and protection through the sword of truth.*

This is extremely effective for your protection. If any type of negative energy should make it past the energy of Michael, it then comes up against the violet flame which transmutes negative energy into love. Should that not be sufficient to stop the remaining energy, the white light of the Christ energy is the final level and will complete the protection. I guarantee that this has worked for me every time and will only let something come into you if you allow it.

# 7

# FRONT LAYOUTS

*"You are made of the stuff of stars. The world needs your light."*

*-Lazaris*

The **front layouts are usually the first layouts clients will experience.** They are less intense than the back layouts and will generally begin to delve into the emotions that cause all dis-eases in the body. It addresses blocks in the energy that usually happen around the chakras. This type of energy work will begin to balance and heal the energies which lays the foundation for higher levels of energy healing. As with most crystal healing sessions, other things might crop up to be looked at or at least brought to the attention.

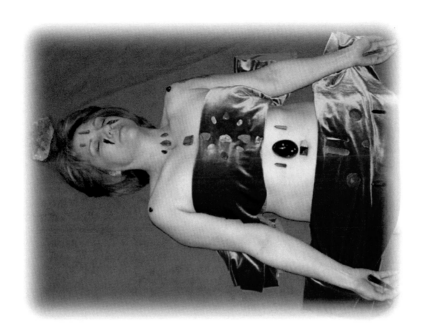

# FULL FRONT LAYOUT

**PURPOSE:** A front layout like this addresses all the chakras and any other issues that might come up. It brings forth blocks in the energy that are reflected in the physical. No two layouts are alike but one might look like this.

**USES:** The Amethyst that lies at the crown chakra will change any negative energy coming in, to love. As Lapis is the highest vibration in the physical, its placement on the third eye chakra will aid in the opening to higher vision. The Azurite on the throat assists in the alignment of the will in all aspects. It is also beneficial for thyroid issues. The color of the thymus resembles the dying embers of a campfire. This chakra carries the energy of the shift in consciousness. Most orange-red crystals are useful here as is the Bustamite pictured and some of the purple stones such as Sugilite. We have pink and green stones in the heart chakra for love and healing. The solar plexus has Obsidian as the main energy to help remove illusion from the truth area. Purple and gold Fluorite are used in the navel chakra in this layout to help dissolve blocks and release excess energy. Ruby is placed at the root chakra with Malachite to begin the journey of raising the energy and the discovery of who you really are, with ease. The wands are used to direct energy in certain directions.

**ANECDOTE:** When someone first comes to me for a layout, their energy usually calls for a front layout. I can usually sense what we will be doing but I use muscle testing to double check. "First physician, do no harm".

# FACE LAYOUT

**PURPOSE:** When doing a front layout, we many times address the sinuses where we often have congestion.

**USES:** The stones placed on the sinuses are often Carborundum crystals. This will remove toxins from the area and generate a healing affect. Sinuses are about old and no longer useful emotions, so we require to let them go. As we do that, the sinus glands usually clear.

**ANECDOTE:** Carborundum is a man-made crystal in most instances. If you took residue from making the large carbon grinding stones and heated it to very high temperatures, you would have a creation like this. I feel it is similar to clinkers created in old coal furnaces. These do have more color to them so something might be added to the process. While I usually steer clear of lab created crystals, some are very useful even if we've created them.

# HEART STONES 1 LAYOUT

**PURPOSE:** This layout utilizes both pink and green stones. It would aid in helping blocked energy in the heart.

**USES:** The pink stones will open the heart to allow the love energy to flow and the green stones help the heart to heal. In the center of the layout is a Rose Quartz cluster. Clusters are quite rare. The other pink stones are tumbled Rose Quartz crystals. The green stones are Aventurine.

**ANECDOTE:** As both of these stones are nearly equal in their vibrations and quite gentle, I would generally be directed to use them on someone who is a novice to energies or who require a gentle opening and healing of the heart vibration.

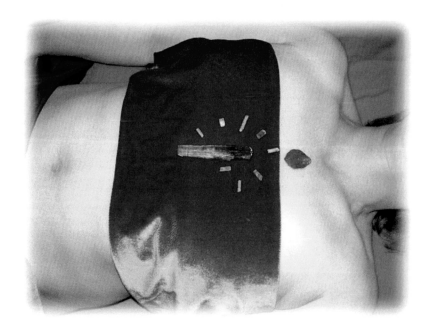

# HEART STONES 2 LAYOUT

**PURPOSE:** This layout of the Tourmaline is to infuse the heart with a higher vibration as it opens. The Sugilite lays on the thymus chakra and aids in bringing the love vibration into this chakra of enlightenment.

**USES:** Tourmaline is truly a heart crystal in all colors. This carries a higher vibration than most of the other pink and green heart stones. The spiral pattern provides an elevation of energy so that those who are ready can increase the heart vibration. Sugilite is also a heart stone but works well with the thymus chakra. This brings a greater understanding as the heart opens.

**ANECDOTE:** The energy of all these crystals is wonderful to work with in the layouts. They are also beneficial for anyone just to sit with to work with heart energy. The frequency is definitely a step up from the frequency of the Rose Quartz, green Aventurine and Kunzite. You would use these in the final stage of opening the heart chakra completely.

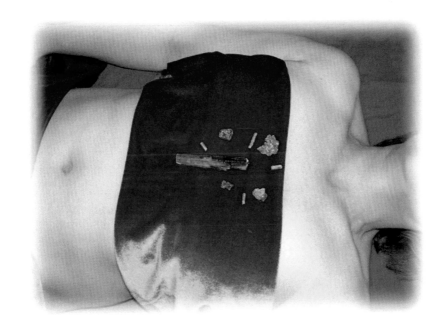

# HEART STONES 3 LAYOUT

**PURPOSE:** Different crystals will take the heart vibration to even greater levels.

**USES:** This layout still uses the pink and green Tourmalines but now includes Wulfenite. This crystal has ten times the intensity of Ruby and Garnet. Wulfenite would be used for hardcore blockage in the heart area for those who are demanding the opening of the heart chakra rather than allowing it. This layout would create a powerful opening. At times, Lapis might be used in place of the Wulfenite for a slightly different vibration.

**ANECDOTE:** As most of us are allowing the healing of the heart energy, all of these crystals would be amazingly helpful. We are all somewhat fearful of what we might find buried within that energy to be healed, but it is a requirement on our journey.

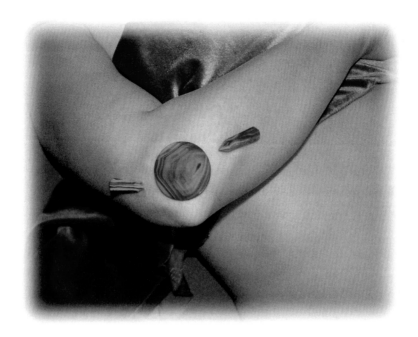

# ELBOW FRONT/BACK LAYOUT

**PURPOSE:** The reason for using the stones in this way would be to address pain and discomfort in the elbow area.

**USES:** Malachite is so useful. It is a stone that would alleviate pain, both mental and physical pain. It would also be very healing as green is the color of healing.

**ANECDOTE:** This is a stone that I use quite often in the healing layouts. When someone finds the energy stuck in a particular place, it often turns to pain due to the resistance to letting go of old energy blocks. This placement may also be used in a back layout.

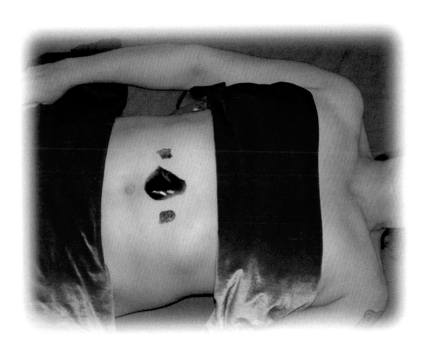

# SOLAR PLEXUS 1 LAYOUT

**PURPOSE:** The solar plexus is the seat of the soul and our truth center. To place stones in this area would assist one to understand what is true and what is illusion. Its color is typically yellow but other crystals may be used to accomplish your goal.

**USES:** I have used Obsidian and Ametrine in this placement. Obsidian is strongly geared to stripping away illusion to expose the truth. Most of humanity is enamored of their illusions and reluctant to give them up, but for those who are ready and will allow, Obsidian would be most helpful. Ametrine is a combination of Amethyst and Citrine. Amethyst will take anything that is negative energy and transmute it to love. Citrine is about truth but will also help to release fear in the process of letting go of the illusions.

**ANECDOTE:** I'm sure most of us have heard the phrase 'gut feeling.' When we have that feeling, it pays to listen to the solar plexus, the gut, the truth. If we ignore it, we just might really regret it. It is easy to work with these crystals. Just sit with them, holding them in the solar plexus area.

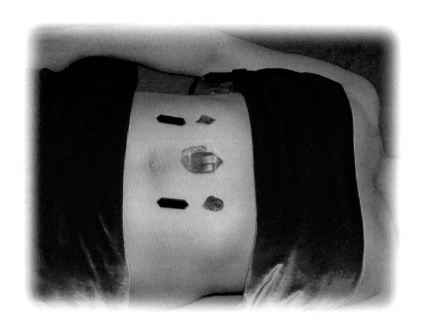

# SOLAR PLEXUS 2 LAYOUT

><<><><><><><><><><><><><><><><><><><><><><><><><><><><><><><><

**PURPOSE:** This photo is an example of the same stones but different shapes and sizes.

**USES:** Here again, we are opening the solar plexus to the truth within us instead of continuing to live in the illusions. The Citrine in the center is emphasizing truth to a greater degree.

**ANECDOTE:** The majority of Citrine is heated to different shades of yellow and orange. The base crystal would probably be an Amethyst of light color. Being both are Quartz crystals, we can still use it for healing. The particular Citrine in this photo happens to be a natural crystal. I really like the energy of these and do find an elevated energy present. The hue of the natural Citrine is usually very light in color.

# ROOT CHAKRA  FRONT/BACK LAYOUT

**PURPOSE:** As with all the chakras, stones are placed to remove blocks and energize the chakra. The stones vary greatly with each person depending on what the issues are. The root chakra is viewed as the base of the kundalini energy and life force.

**USES:** This particular layout contains Malachite, Lepidolite and gold Fluorite. If I were led to place Malachite there, I would understand that there was a great deal of pain present. The Lepidolite contains lithium, so it would bring ease to the situation. The gold color of Fluorite is very intense and would break up stubborn blocks there.

**ANECDOTE:** The placement of the stones is a very intuitive process. No two layouts are the same. Sometimes, I'm not sure why a certain stone is placed in a specific area. But I trust my guidance and I ask for the highest good to be done in every layout.

# 8

# STONES & CRYSTALS

*The soul is like a crystal with hundreds of facets and can manifest in
hundreds of ways at once.*

**All of the stones and crystals carry a unique energy that can be accessed for
our healing.** Yes, they do have special uses but keep in mind that your intent
has a lot to do with how they work. If you feel drawn to a stone, it is probably
one that matches your energy and that you can work with at that time. The following
pages will help you to understand how to identify them and use them and will give
you an idea of the level of energy that I would associate with them.

# ACTINOLITE

**CRYSTAL DESCRIPTION:** Actinolite is a silicate mineral. The color is light to blackish green and goes from transparent to nearly opaque. It is a close relative of Jade.

**USES:** This stone raises the vibratory rate of the entire being. It would be especially beneficial for the heart chakra. It allows an integration of new awareness gained and a connection with 'All-That-Is.' If you would take Serpentine, Kunzite and a little energy of Hematite and bring them all together to transform the heart by expanding the love, you would have the energy Actinolite.

**ANECDOTE:** For those of you who are seeking to expand the love within, Actinolite would help you to achieve that.

**ENERGY LEVEL:**

# AGATE-BLUE LACE

**CRYSTAL DESCRIPTION:** Blue Lace Agate is various shades of blue and banded.

**USES:** Blue Lace Agate sweetens the will and also enhances the ability to tell the truth. It will also open the will to inner vision. It is not powerful as in the dynamic of blasting through any blockages but a gently flow almost like Lepidolite.

**ANECDOTE:** Don't you just love it when the Masters phrase the definition as the ability to tell the truth instead of stopping the lie? That is what I would call positive phrasing!

**ENERGY LEVEL:**

# AGATE-MOSS

**CRYSTAL DESCRIPTION:** Moss Agate is a stone that looks like it has green moss within. It generally forms with white agate inside.

**USES:** The Moss Agate is an indicator of translations of energies. It has a grounding property and yet it is also about severing the ties of bondage to issues and concepts that no long fit in this place. It is unveiling or creating a sense of freedom in areas that have long been limited, blocked or hidden. As the liberation occurs, this stone holds the entity in the body. It would keep the mind and the etheric energy grounded in the body for the presence of life. This would be used on the knees, ankles and pelvic areas and then, for balance, perhaps place it on the third eye or on the temples.

**ANECDOTE:** Agates are so plentiful that we tend to think of them as not particularly helpful. There are so many patterns and colors available that it is amazing. But every stone and crystal has a specific energy and all of them can aid us in our healing.

**ENERGY LEVEL:** 〔〕〔〕

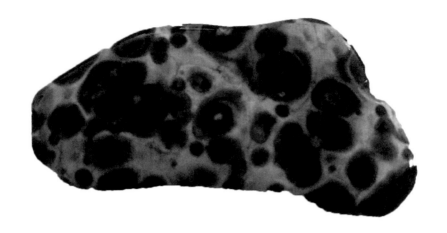

# AGATE-LEOPARDSKIN

**CRYSTAL DESCRIPTION:** This Agate occurs in a variation of colors but all have the spots.

**USES:** Leopardskin Agate is a stone for aligning power. If you were to use this on the front of the body, you would use it in the center between the navel and the pelvic bone, preferably with one stone on each point of the pelvis. Obsidian and clear Quartz add to the power of the stone.

**ANECDOTE:** There are many varieties of Agate and they are actually a microcrystalline variety of Quartz. The Leopardskin Agate isn't as powerful as some stones, but it will get the job done!

**ENERGY LEVEL:**

# AMAZONITE

**CRYSTAL DESCRIPTION:** Amazonite is a beautiful turquoise color. It is an Alkali Feldspar. It can be transparent to translucent and it sometimes has quite a pearly luster.

**USES:** Amazonite brings the masculine and feminine into balance and brings one into the allowance of the intuitive. In these times, Amazonite is becoming more and more a stone of wisdom and emotional healing. It delves into the mysteries and draws out old emotion to be healed. It will help to maintain the balance of fluids in the body.

**ANECDOTE:** In Colorado, the miners are excavating Amazonite with dark Smoky Quartz crystals growing into it. That is an amazing combination.

**ENERGY LEVEL:**

# AMBLYGONITE

**CRYSTAL DESCRIPTION:** Amblygonite is a crystal that can range from transparent to translucent and can occur in several different colors: white to grayish white, pinkish, colorless, yellowish, greenish and bluish.

**USES:** Amblygonite contains high levels of lithium and will bond love and peace and the willingness to allow them. This would be especially helpful for those who are confused in the mind or overly passionate. It might be worn by those who will be in litigation or involved with the law in some trying way.

**ANECDOTE:** I feel everyone would like to experience the energy of love and peace within them. But, we have to allow that to come to us and aid us in our future ongoing.

**ENERGY LEVEL:** ⬡ ⬡

# AMEGREEN

**CRYSTAL DESCRIPTION:** Amegreen is a purple and green color. It's actually a combination of purple and green Amethyst. The green is called Prasiolite. Both are Quartz crystals and can range from transparent to translucent.

**USES:** Amegreen ignites the light that the soul is about through all of creation. This ignites the remembering of that brilliance within self that has been so dimmed by the illusion. It provides the light that the mind could not even imagine if it meditated upon it, for the mind could not imagine going into places of that crystalline clarity or that absolute unimpeded vision. It is most definitely a stone of remembering.

**ANECDOTE:** I do like working with this stone. It triggers an energy that calls deeply to us.

**ENERGY LEVEL:** ◊ ◊ ◊

# AMETHYST

**CRYSTAL DESCRIPTION:** Amethyst is an awesome purple color. It is usually transparent and is in the quartz family.

**USES:** Amethyst is the alchemist of stones and therefore it transmutes negative energy into love. It aids the digestion, which sweetens the belly, purifies the understanding and relieves the mind, somewhat, of trauma because it is alchemical. It reduces stress and would help one to think clearly and to express those thoughts.

**ANECDOTE:** Amethyst is a stone I use often because it is so good about changing negative thoughts. It is associated with the violet flame so when I have negative thoughts I can put them into the flame and transmute them. And I do have negative thoughts sometimes and really do not want to create them in the physical!

**ENERGY LEVEL:**

# AMETRINE

**CRYSTAL DESCRIPTION:** Another of the Quartz crystals, Ametrine is a combination of Amethyst and Citrine so it is purple and gold colored.

**USES:** The gold and purple colors of the Ametrine signify that wisdom has combined with the overcoming of karma. This is the bonding of wisdom with truth, with the Higher Self, with the allowing of all that you are, God-Goddess-All-That-Is, Higher Self, God Within. This is the bonding of the little self (ego) with the Great Self. It is how truth is now presented. Traces of the Higher Self are now expressing in the wisdom zone for the bonding of self with Self so that your little self is not so terrified to realize your Higher Self always loved you.

**ANECDOTE:** I have used Ametrine many times in the solar plexus chakra, the truth center, for the bonding within which we all require.

**ENERGY LEVEL:** ⬡ ⬡ ⬡

# ANGELITE

**CRYSTAL DESCRIPTION:** Angelite is a beautiful sky-blue color. It is found on the Nazca Plain in Peru.

**USES:** Angelite is of the divine mind. It helps connect the right and left sides of the brain and activates the right brain. Where this once was an excessively high frequency that only a few could tolerate, it is now not necessarily ordinary but certainly fits into the mundane much more easily than it has in the past. Now, this is something that would probably be good for most anyone, anywhere.

**ANECDOTE:** When the right and left sides of my brain began to make the connection, I experienced some discomfort. I feel Angelite will help to make the connection easier.

**ENERGY LEVEL:**

# APATITE

**CRYSTAL DESCRIPTION:** Apatite occurs in several colors including yellow, blue and neon blue-green. One of the phosphates, it is transparent to translucent.

**USES:** Apatite literally deals with our appetites. It will assist humanity to overcome addictions and compulsions. It will ease the stress of the addictions and causes a sense of being full so there is not the hunger of lack. The dark blue goes even beyond the other colors. It is an awakening for those who are willing to begin to feel that empowerment again of just how vastly important it is that spirit is the guiding force of the life and not the mind. The energy can flow from above to below and it is like electricity, information that flows like water so it is in many ways a combination of fire, air and water informing matter.

**ANECDOTE:** I dare say all of us have some kind of addiction. We usually develop these as a way to stay grounded. But another thing addiction does is to keep us from our connection to spirit. So, stones of this type are very helpful in that regard.

**ENERGY LEVEL:**

# AQUAMARINE

**CRYSTAL DESCRIPTION:** Aquamarine is an amazing blue and usually transparent. It belongs to the beryl family of gems and is a silicate.

**USES:** Ascendancy is gained by freedom, freedom from entrapment of the illusion of emotion. This is a freedom stone, a stone of purity. The purity of purpose assists the freedom. It promotes freedom for those who feel trapped.

**ANECDOTE:** While most gemstones carry a very high frequency, for what this assists us in doing, I gave it a level one energy.

**ENERGY LEVEL:**

# ATACAMITE

CRYSTAL DESCRIPTION: Atacamite can be translucent to transparent. The color varies from bright green to very dark green. This forms in the oxidized regions of copper deposits, as a secondary mineral, in association with Malachite, Azurite and Quartz.

USES: Atacamite dispenses joy in a magnified way. Joy vibrates in the cellular structure of the physical body and so, as this would be meditated upon or worn upon the body, it would bring into the physical affairs, into the daily life a greater sense of joy, delight with being and a greater sense of well-being. It would assist in sweetening the emotional nature and uplifting the heart and the mind and making the sense of joy real in this illusion.

ANECDOTE: Who couldn't use a little or maybe a lot, of joy in their lives? This energy is a pleasure to work with.

ENERGY LEVEL: ▯

# AVENTURINE

**CRYSTAL DESCRIPTION:** Aventurine is actually a variety of Quartz. It often has a grainy texture.

**USES:** Green Aventurine is primarily a heart stone. It may be used with Rose Quartz in the heart area when gentle energy is called for. This helps to gently heal the heart and unites the heart and soul. Blue Aventurine addresses the wounded healer in every being. This would begin to pull the veil aside so that there is a greater ease and capability to function in higher frequencies. The blue works well with the third eye chakra. Red Aventurine works as a connector between the solar plexus chakra and the thymus chakra. It helps open the energy of the heart to all the perfection of spirit to flow through where wounded hearts could not bear it.

**ANECDOTE:** As my family and I were hunting rocks and found Aventurine, we called it sugar stone because it shone like sugar in the sunlight.

**ENERGY LEVEL:** Green ⬦   Blue ⬦ ⬦ ⬦   Red ⬦ ⬦ ⬦

# AZURITE

CRYSTAL DESCRIPTION: Azurite is usually a rich, deep azure blue. It forms as crystals, massive or nodules. This is also a crystal that forms in the oxidized regions of copper deposits. It is a carbonate.

USES: Azurite relates to the refining energy of the Higher Self and works on alignment of the will in all aspects. 'I will change my mind. I will shift my position. I will change my perspective.' One would use this where there are blocks to flexibility.

ANECDOTE: I often use this in the throat chakra to address the will issues.

ENERGY LEVEL: ▯

# BARITE

**CRYSTAL DESCRIPTION:** Barite can have many different colors and is transparent to translucent. It is a sulfate.

**USES:** Barite has a high spiritual energy and rapidly eliminates fear. It can be used for cutting away fear and limitation when one is truly seeking the God-self.

**ANECDOTE:** Barite is a crystal that is so useful. As we all carry fear, we could use a crystal that would help us deal with it!

**ENERGY LEVEL:** 🔹 🔹

# BISMUTH

**CRYSTAL DESCRIPTION:** Bismuth is a high-density, silvery, pink-tinged metal. It is brittle and so it is usually mixed with other metals to make it useful. It's alloys with tin or cadmium have low melting points and are used in fire detectors and extinguishers, electric fuses and solders. The addition of the other elements to Bismuth create a variety of colors when heated in a lab.

**USES:** On a mundane level, Bismuth can actually act energetically on the body very much like an antibiotic. It's almost as though, as the veil slides aside, there are those who will get messages encoded in concepts like reading a schematic or receiving a very intricately encoded message. To those who are responsive to this stone, it will begin to open up new levels of technology that assist in going beyond physicality: in the world but not of it, moving in a physical form but not trapped by its density. It can be, for those who are willing even if they don't believe it, an assist in connecting body and soul, mind and soul, physicality and soul so that there is an acceptance in the physical daily affairs that there's a lot more to this than what the eye can see and the ear can hear.

**ANECDOTE:** Even though this is an alloy, you can see that this might be very helpful to connect us in such a way that we become more whole within ourselves. Bismuth would act as an antibiotic much like Peacock Ore.

**ENERGY LEVEL:** ⬙⬙

# BLOODSTONE

**CRYSTAL DESCRIPTION:** Bloodstone is a mix of stones. It is dense in its make-up.

**USES:** Bloodstone is literally a blood purifier. It is very much of the physical body but bridges into the essential levels.

**ANECDOTE:** There is a legend that says that when Jesus was on the cross and blood dripped from His wound onto the rock below, bloodstone was created.

**ENERGY LEVEL:**

# BUDDSTONE

**CRYSTAL DESCRIPTION:** The coloration of this stone is a unique green. It is likely a Jasper.

**USES:** Buddstone assists beings to remember that they are becoming who they really are. When worn on the body it will gently peel away limitations and all the resistances to the mastery. It carries the purifying properties of Bloodstone and the soothing healing qualities of Jade.

**ANECDOTE:** We do tend to treat ourselves badly. When we don't feel good enough, we put up limitations of all kinds. When we speak of allowing, that requires the breaking down of limits that keep us from all the riches that are our divine inheritance. And that means treating ourselves gently and with respect.

**ENERGY LEVEL:** ⧫ ⧫

# BUSTAMITE

**CRYSTAL DESCRIPTION:** Bustamite is an opaque stone that usually forms in masses. It's color ranges from light pink to a reddish brown. It is thought to be closely related to Rhodonite.

**USES:** Bustamite is associated with the thymus chakra and has to do with the energies of ascendancy. It is a birthing force of new understanding of self and the assistance of aligning the will in love. It is very subtle in its ongoing, a stone that would assist those who will be drawn to it to move into greater energetic allowing of ascension.

**ANECDOTE:** I frequently use Bustamite in my layouts. The thymus chakra is the energy of the shift in consciousness and this stone would take us into that energy or at least give us some insight of what can be accomplished in the higher frequencies if we allow it. The awesome color of the thymus chakra is that of the dying embers of a campfire. It glows.

**ENERGY LEVEL:**

# CACOXINITE

**CRYSTAL DESCRIPTION:** Cacoxinite is a stone made up of Quartz and filaments of other minerals. It can range in color from brownish to yellow.

**USES:** Cacoxinite is a crystal that soothes the emotions and assists the digestion. It is the cauldron of alchemy. This would have a Plutonian nature of the deepest, most internal places of the self, of the earth. It would assist in bringing those who are very close to getting the vision of creation into a place of understanding how it is.

**ANECDOTE:** This is such a wonderful stone. A lot of them have a hint of Amethyst in them.

**ENERGY LEVEL:**

# CALCITE

∽∽∽∽∽∽∽∽∽∽∽∽∽∽∽∽∽∽∽∽∽∽∽∽∽∽∽∽∽∽∽∽∽∽∽∽

**CRYSTAL DESCRIPTION:** Calcite is a carbonate and has several different forms including optical, dogtooth and nail head. There is a wide range of colors.

**USES:** Most Calcites deal with the stabilizing of emotions. All of the colors, aside from the green and Cobalto, may be used most effectively in the bath. The different colors will assist, more or less, in different ways. Several of the colors may aid in embracing prosperity on all levels. These include the orange and peach stones. The Cobalto Calcite would probably fit into that category, also. The Cobalto also assists one to bear it when one has opened the door to a new awareness. The white is the strongest of the colors and aids in clearing and purifying the physical body. To accomplish this, bathe with it for thirty minutes. The yellow Calcite has to do with the dispelling of fear, the releasing of wisdom and the assistance of the remembering.

**ANECDOTE:** As you can see, all the Calcites can be very helpful as we deal with all things from emotional to the physical, from prosperity to enlightenment.

**ENERGY LEVEL:**
Blue, Green, Peach, White, Yellow     Orange ⬨ ⬨    Cobalto ⬨ ⬨ ⬨

∽∽∽∽∽∽∽∽∽∽∽∽∽∽∽∽∽∽∽∽∽∽∽∽∽∽∽∽∽∽∽∽∽∽∽∽∽

# CARBORUNDUM

CRYSTAL DESCRIPTION: This crystal is typically man-made. A base mineral is taken and is heated to a high temperature. The result is this amazing stone.

USES: Carborundum works upon the body much like an air purifier works upon the ozone. It draws toxins forth and catches most of the toxicity so that what passes through will not contaminate the air around the body as the body is cleared. It has an antibiotic effect much like Peacock Ore. As toxins are pulled out, antibiotic energy is put in to deal with infections.

ANECDOTE: I'm not sure if this occurs naturally or not. I have a piece that I was told by a rockhound came out of a place of volcanic activity. Regardless, it could be a helpful addition to our healing.

ENERGY LEVEL:

# CARNELIAN

**CRYSTAL DESCRIPTION:** Carnelian is the orange variety of Quartz. It ranges light to dark orange and is usually transparent.

**USES:** Carnelian assists coming to power because it assists in setting fear aside. It allows more of the focus on power and clearer understanding of what power really is, for the misconceptions of power have been very much intertwined with the misconceptions of separation here. Carnelian assists one in coming to their power, feeling the power or feeling the misalignments where the connections are not made. It aids them in reconnecting to their power.

**ANECDOTE:** All the stones are accelerating in their energy. This is no exception. There is a dark rich orange color of Carnelian that would go a long way to seat the energy into the power center. This would be the true essence of Carnelian.

**ENERGY LEVEL:**

# CELESTITE

**CRYSTAL DESCRIPTION:** Celestite is a sulfate and forms in a variety of colors. This sky-blue color seems to be the most common. It is transparent to translucent and often grows in hydrothermal veins.

**USES:** Celestite has an exquisitely high frequency and refined energy. It brings wisdom of higher places and it cleanses. This will give you a clearer and clearer sense of your own largesse, your ability to command authority and power, not by dominance but by alignment with higher force. The power that you create, celestial, celestine, the ability to align with spirit, isn't something over there. The stones such as Angelite and Celestite are helping to bring integration, in the world but not of it.

**ANECDOTE:** What an amazing crystal! Celestite is a sky-blue crystal that will take us beyond where we have ever been. The future before us has nothing relating to the past. Its completely unexplored territory.

**ENERGY LEVEL:** ▯ ▯ ▯

# CHAROITE

CRYSTAL DESCRIPTION: Charoite is a purple stone and is often found with Aergirine and Orthoclase. No crystal shape has been found. It can be transparent or translucent. The only place in the world it is found is in Siberia.

USES: The equation of the balanced mind, this stone reduces the illusion and draws in the understanding of the magik of the universe. The Grand Force is neither dark nor light, it is all. Man has feared the darkness but the Great Void, the Mystery, is a place of darkness as the womb is a place of darkness. That is why man has feared it so. It is hidden, a mystery. Man will open to his own understanding of that mystery, that void, and it will not be so fearsome, it will be awesome.

ANECDOTE: This is one of those stones that has a very high frequency. We didn't begin to get much of the Charoite until tensions eased with the eastern bloc countries. Charoite can be carved and it was used as vases and other decorative items.

ENERGY LEVEL: ▯ ▯ ▯

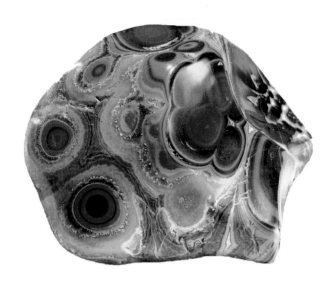

# CHRYSOCOLLA/MALACHITE

**CRYSTAL DESCRIPTION:** The minerals in this combination are both formed in the oxidation zone of copper deposits. Chrysocolla and Malachite can be translucent to opaque.

**USES:** Chrysocolla/Malachite contains the grounding of the very powerful pain relief of the Malachite but also a great deal of soothing and healing for what we may call the wounded soul. This would address dis-easement on all levels. It would assist with pain in the physical form because the pain comes from the unseen levels. It would assist in repairing a much frayed nervous system. It would help in an alignment that would heal the wounds of separation. So, it is a mending, blending, unifying, healing stone that would bring mighty healing. It truly is an aggressive healer.

**ANECDOTE:** Sometimes called Malacolla, this is a wonderful stone to work with as sometimes our resistance to letting go of our challenges causes pain.

**ENERGY LEVEL:**

# CHRYSOPRASE

**CRYSTAL DESCRIPTION:** Chrysoprase is the green variety of Chalcedony. It can be transparent to opaque and is often found where there has been volcanic activity. It can also be formed as a dehydration product of Opal.

**USES:** Chrysoprase has to do with the alignment of the divine androgyny. It assists in bonding of masculine and feminine energies in a more peaceful manner. The nature of the energy of Chrysoprase is a blend of the energies of Turquoise, Azurite and Malachite.

**ANECDOTE:** As we are all on a path to divine androgyny, when we are at the point of allowing that process, the Chrysoprase would be a good stone to turn to.

**ENERGY LEVEL:**

# CITRINE

〰〰〰〰〰〰〰〰〰〰〰〰〰〰〰〰〰〰〰〰〰〰〰〰

**CRYSTAL DESCRIPTION:** Citrine is found in abundance in Brazil. The majority of what we can purchase is heat treated Amethyst to produce the yellow, orange and brownish colors. Citrine is a Quartz variety and hexagonal. Some natural, not heated, is available but is very light in color.

**USES:** Yellow Citrine promotes the energy of truth. It is an excellent stone to help the kidneys when there is a tendency to ticked off. A great deal of the planet is experiencing this in these times. Citrine would be very helpful in alleviating the sense of being overly angry or fearfully angry. Fear and anger are great companions and so the Citrine would definitely help to alleviate all manner of fear. Citrine is a wonderfully beautiful stone for bringing a sense of clarity in the midst of irrational anger.

**ANECDOTE:** I've found that even if the Citrine has been heat treated, it works well. I do like the natural Citrine for it's higher energy.

**ENERGY LEVEL:** ⬡

〰〰〰〰〰〰〰〰〰〰〰〰〰〰〰〰〰〰〰〰〰〰〰〰

# CITRON

<<<<<<<<<<<<<<<<<<<<<<<<<<<<<<<<<<<<<<<<<<<<<<<<<<<<<<<<<<<

**CRYSTAL DESCRIPTION:** This stone is sometimes referred to as lemon Chrysoprase. It varies in its color from Chrysoprase and is opaque. This would be classed as Chalcedony.

**USES:** The frequency with which this stone is associated is an example of how the energies work. Citron will assist in the remembering of how the primal understanding, the very basic primal understanding of the earth is enlightened and illuminated.

**ANECDOTE:** The color is so soft in this stone. In addition to the above uses, it is full of stories of what has been. It can be a blessing or a curse. If a being desires to remember, it will assist them to remember. If they only thought they wanted to remember, this will open a Pandora's box for them.

**ENERGY LEVEL:** ▯

# CROCOITE

**CRYSTAL DESCRIPTION:** Crocoite is primarily a bright orange-red. It is a chromate that forms in the oxidized zone of veins and deposits containing Chromium and Lead. Crocoite is a secondary mineral, resulting from the alteration of other Lead minerals by hydrothermal fluids.

**USES:** When used on the thymus chakra, the Christ consciousness, inner energy is intensified because the Christ color is the red of the rose. This will bond the Christ consciousness to the root, primal force brought into the awareness of the God-self. It helps man open to his remembering that what he calls miracles is not.

**ANECDOTE:** Crocoite is such a beautiful crystal. It's energy is high and so helpful. It comes from Australia.

**ENERGY LEVEL:** ⬙ ⬙ ⬙

# DIASPORE

∞∞∞∞∞∞∞∞∞∞∞∞∞∞∞∞∞∞∞∞∞∞∞∞∞∞∞∞∞∞∞∞∞∞∞

**CRYSTAL DESCRIPTION:** Diaspore often forms in blades and ranges from light to dark brown. There are other colors but the brown seems to be most common. It can be transparent or translucent. It is a hydroxide.

**USES:** Diaspore is for those with war-like tendencies, attitudes and concepts that have existed in places like the Holy Land. It assists those who have come from such places many times, those who carry those attitudes, those energies, that understanding. It helps to purify, to rapidly cleanse warlike tendencies.

**ANECDOTE:** The first time I saw this crystal, someone handed me a blade of it. The color looked like Smoky Quartz but the shape was wrong and the energy was certainly different. I was really drawn to it and I wouldn't rule out the fact that I have war-like tendencies sometimes!

**ENERGY LEVEL:**

∞∞∞∞∞∞∞∞∞∞∞∞∞∞∞∞∞∞∞∞∞∞∞∞∞∞∞∞∞∞∞∞∞∞∞

# DIOPTASE

∞∞∞∞∞∞∞∞∞∞∞∞∞∞∞∞∞∞∞∞∞∞∞∞∞∞∞∞∞∞∞∞∞∞∞∞∞∞∞∞∞

**CRYSTAL DESCRIPTION:** Dioptase is a striking emerald to deep bluish green. It can be transparent to translucent. This crystal occurs where copper veins have been altered by oxidation. It can also be found in hollows and cavities in surrounding rocks. It is a silicate.

**USES:** Dioptase amplifies joy. A little is a lot because man is not accustomed to joy. One might use this in the adrenals with Citrine to alleviate fear and bring a more delightful encounter with life.

**ANECDOTE:** I am so drawn to the color of this crystal. I find I use it quite often in the layouts that I do because we can all use a little more joy in our lives.

**ENERGY LEVEL:**

# DOLOMITE

**CRYSTAL DESCRIPTION:** Dolomite occurs in various colors that include colorless, white, gray, pinkish and brown. It has almost a pearly luster and ranges from transparent to translucent. It forms in hydrothermal veins and in magnesium limestones.

**USES:** Dolomite is an interesting crystal that carries an essence almost beyond words in our language. To say it is cleansing is almost too abrasive, to say it is purifying is too astringent because of the love in it. It draws down the white light and brings that energy through the lower body, the belly, hips and legs so the lower body might be connected, for man has a tendency to ground through the low body and it becomes a muck. Dolomite gently restores order and assists those afraid of their power to come to terms with it little by little rather than getting all the power and understanding at once.

**ANECDOTE:** It is time to embrace our empowerment, to step into it regardless of the fear. Of all the crystals, this would likely be the most gentle in helping you to achieve that.

**ENERGY LEVEL:**

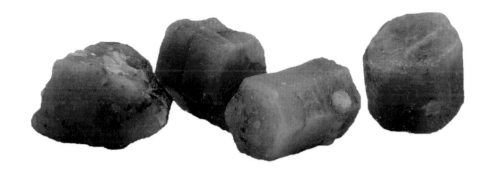

# EMERALD

**CRYSTAL DESCRIPTION:** Emerald is a Beryl and is transparent to translucent. It forms in pegmatites and granites and in some metamorphosed rocks.

**USES:** Emerald is a gemstone that is used not only in the heart but also somewhat in the throat to raise the purity of the truth into the will area. Because the nature of the heart is changing, the nature of the Emerald is being influenced and as it is accepted and integrated, the energy of the Emerald opens self to depths of psycho-spiritual elements where the psyche and the spirit begin to blend as intellect or the intelligent mind begins to transform and is revealed to the much greater aspects of itself. Emerald is the royal stone of the heart. It assists in these times when the heart is opening to much higher levels of understanding.

**ANECDOTE:** As with all of the green stones, Emerald is a valuable tool to aid in the healing of all the afflictions we experience.

**ENERGY LEVEL:** 🔋 🔋

# EPIDOTE

**CRYSTAL DESCRIPTION:** Epidote is a silicate that ranges from yellowish green to green, brownish green to greenish black to black. It is usually transparent to nearly opaque. It forms in metamorphic and igneous rock. It can be fan shaped or barrel shaped which is more crystalline.

**USES:** Considering the conditions of the times, it is good to remember 'peaceful warrior.' Epidote brings the remembering through cellular soul memory. Wisdom is being at one with your God-self and forgiving any warlike destructive thoughts toward yourself or any other. Epidote is a reminder for those who are particularly warlike, for it has a peaceful grounding effect but not tranquilization for tranquility can almost lead to a sleep state. Serenity leads to the peace that allows the listening for the future ongoing. Epidote works more with serenity and paying attention to divine action. Pay attention to your emotions and the challenges you are dealing with. Remember, the strife of life overcomes life!

**ANECDOTE:** There are so many caught up in the violence and chaos of the world in our times. It would be well to remember that there is a divine plan and out of chaos arises creation.

**ENERGY LEVEL:**

# FLUORITE

**CRYSTAL DESCRIPTION:** Fluorite forms in many colors, blue, green, violet, white and yellow. Its cleavage produces octahedrons but there are also many beautiful clusters. This can be found in hydrothermal veins as well as hot springs areas.

**USES:** In general, Fluorite can be used for many things. It clears the etheric body of old blocks and the aura of any problems. The different colors move the energy in different ways. When used with Rose Quartz, the blue Fluorite helps to repair holes or tears in the aura. Green Fluorite would stimulate growth and healing. Violet is an astringent cleanser and works well for removing riders from the aura and releasing a buildup of energy. The white Fluorite balances energy and holds or centers energy in a certain area if placed on either side of where you want that energy centered. Be sure you know what you are holding in one place as the energy is magnified and concentrated. Yellow is the strongest of the colors and may be used anywhere on the body to dissolve blocks.

**ANECDOTE:** Although I love and appreciate all of the stones I work with, Fluorite is my favorite. I feel that is because of the many colors and uses but also its energy is sharp. I really do relate to that. One caution with Fluorite. Don't wear it on your body for long periods of time because the energy will lacerate the aura.

**ENERGY LEVEL:**

# FLUORITE / AMETHYST

**CRYSTAL DESCRIPTION:** This combination of Fluorite and Amethyst could be many different colors as it is common for Fluorite to form with Quartz. Both minerals occur in many colors. Both can form in hydrothermal veins and hot springs.

**USES:** This combination works with transformational cleansing or bringing energies that have been somewhat murky or confused into a point of greater wisdom with what is going on. Fluorite is excellent for cleansing the auric field, the energy around the body, even, perhaps, that which is in a place that doesn't feel particularly good and Amethyst is about the transformational process and bringing thing up to a higher level of frequency.

**ANECDOTE:** The colors of this crystal are soft and the energy is very inviting. I like working with both crystals separately and the combination makes it much nicer.

**ENERGY LEVEL:**

# FUCHSITE

**CRYSTAL DESCRIPTION:** Closely related to Muscovite, Fuchsite ranges from a light bluish color to green. It can be transparent or translucent and has a silky feel to it. This can be found in pegmatites. It contains Mica which gives it a mother-of-pearl appearance.

**USES:** Fuchsite can be an emotional soother because it tends to lift the roiling emotion out of the solar plexus and raise it to higher levels of consciousness so that it can be viewed, not intellectually because that is a resistance to it, but with greater mental clarity. It eases the heart and so, for those who are remembering old emotional wounds, it would be very helpful for the heart. It aids those who have had a lost love, whether by death or divorce or my lover just disappeared, that kind of thing. Fuchsite would be very soothing for the heart and because it brings balance in the emotions, it helps to take all of the irrational fear out of the situation, especially those situations where love, as humanity has understood it, is involved.

**ANECDOTE:** Fuchsite sounds like a stone that we all could use at one time or another. I could have used it years ago!

**ENERGY LEVEL:**

# GARNET

**CRYSTAL DESCRIPTION:** Garnet is a gemstone we tend to think of as red. Actually, it can occur in every color except blue. It is generally transparent to opaque.

**USES:** Each color of Garnet works in different ways. Green Garnet would call in the bonding of the heart and soul together. It gets you into the heart places, into the things you have loved that you were afraid you had lost and that you still fear that you could not go on without even though they were other lifetimes. This color will strongly assist in cutting those ties to lifetimes that no longer serve you. The peach color of Garnet would be excellent for one doing the exercise of calling the light and calling all of their power back to themselves. It would help to hold the frequency of reclamation and owning of one's own power. The deep red colors ground the life force and bring life energy from the base up. Finally, Uvarovite is an Emerald green Garnet from Russia. It takes the fire of the root chakra and brings it more into the universality of love. This brings up the fiery creation of the root and brings an essential opening expression to the heart. Love how you are in this moment rather than attempting to jump a step beyond your humanity to wondrous, spiritual God. To recognize your God, you must love your humanity.

**ANECDOTE:** There are many places in the U.S. where there are Garnets. I find the red ones are more prevalent and sometimes you luck out and find a large one!

**ENERGY LEVEL:**

# HEMATITE

**CRYSTAL DESCRIPTION:** Hematite is the mineral form of iron oxide, one of several iron oxides. It is the oldest known iron oxide mineral that has ever formed on earth and is widespread in rocks and soils. It ranges in color from black to steel or silver-gray, brown to reddish brown or red.

**USES:** Hematite originated on an unnamed blue planet rather like Kyanite. It may be used for grounding or to mirror what you are required to look at. When used in a meditative way, Hematite can connect you with those from other dimensions, those who are called extra-terrestrials, those who have come from other vibrational dimensions. Therefore, this stone is very good about bringing people back into their bodies which is vitally important in this time because most of humanity is not in their body below the heart chakra. And so, Hematite brings them back into the body in a solid way so that they can face what they are attempting to escape. Hematite is not only about grounding but also for protection. As I return to my body, I am safe there and then, as I am in my body, I can open that spiritual ear gate to communicate with those from higher dimensional frequencies.

**ANECDOTE:** Hematite was known as Bloodstone in earlier times because, as it was cut, the water used turned red from the iron in it. While most of the people I know use it for grounding, we are being given new and different ways to interact with its energy.

**ENERGY LEVEL:**

# HEMATITE-RAINBOW

**CRYSTAL DESCRIPTION:** Rainbow Hematite is an iron ore covered with a natural coating of aluminum phosphate nanoparticles which gives it a rainbow iridescence.

**USES:** More and more we are calling in the universal energies of One. On earth, Hematite is grounding so it calls itself in from the stars. It is an essence, a symbol, an aspect of the rainbow bridge. All Are One!

**ANECDOTE:** When I first purchased these stones, most people thought they were man-created. These are completely natural and very beautiful.

**ENERGY LEVEL:** 🔹 🔹 🔹

# HEMIMORPHITE

**CRYSTAL DESCRIPTION:** Hemimorphite occurs in many colors including white, blue, green, gray, yellowish and brown. It forms where zinc veins have been changed by oxidation. This is another of the silicates.

**USES:** Hemimorphite is a stone for those who are reaching very rapidly into their becoming. It is the essence of the beginning of life and how it becomes cellularly from a concept, like a starburst, like a nova. It is as if it has come full circle, from God to God. It is to remind one of the completed circle. This will revitalize the opening of the pineal and the pituitary so that it is clean and clear, for there are those who are opening who are still foggy in their vision.

**ANECDOTE:** The energy of Hemimorphite is compelling. The blue color of this is especially striking.

**ENERGY LEVEL:** 〇 〇 〇

# HERKIMER DIAMOND

**CRYSTAL DESCRIPTION:** Herkimer Diamonds are Quartz crystals that are double terminated. Most are extremely clear. These form in pockets of solid rock. They are named for Herkimer, New York where it is found.

**USES:** The Herkimer Diamond will be extremely assertive in those that would be really committed to connecting to their divine inheritance. Rich! The rage against rich. This would assist in delving into understanding and overcoming the rage and fear of truly being wealthy. The healing properties would address all levels: physical, mental, emotional and spiritual. But the wholeness of the energy would be the reconnection to the divine inheritance.

**ANECDOTE:** Humankind has no idea how we block our prosperity by using negative thoughts and words. Does the term 'filthy rich' sound familiar? How about, 'I wonder how many people he climbed over to get his money? He sure didn't work for it.' Instead, ask yourself, "How does it feel to be a millionaire?" When you judge others, you judge yourself and effectively block your prosperity.

**ENERGY LEVEL:**

# HIDDENITE

**CRYSTAL DESCRIPTION:** Hiddenite is of the Spodumene family. The colors of these crystals vary widely and can be transparent to translucent. They are found in granite pegmatites. Most of the Spodumene carry lithium.

**USES:** Hiddenite is used to open the heart and recognize the love there which is not necessarily enjoyable. Much like Dioptase, this allows the joy of the love, the delight of the love, the bubble. When used with pink Kunzite, they would not only be informed, they would be delighted to know!

**ANECDOTE:** A lot of Hiddenite is an Emerald green. The ones I've seen are more of a soft green. I feel that anything that can aid in the opening of the heart is something to explore.

**ENERGY LEVEL:**

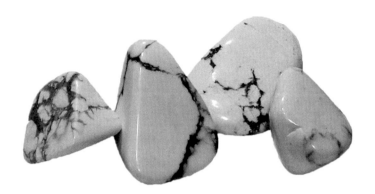

# HOWLITE

**CRYSTAL DESCRIPTION:** Howlite is a borate mineral found in evaporate areas. It is usually white with veins of black, gray or brown. It is an opaque stone.

**USES:** Representative of the temples of Atlantis, it has to do with calling those who are from those places and times to be at peace with their creations. It is purity and yet it has a veining of darkness. It allows that the mixture is all right.

**ANECDOTE:** Howlite can be dyed and misrepresented as Turquoise. Find a reputable dealer who will be open about what you are actually buying. And yes, the continent of Atlantis did exist. Many of the beings there were involved in DNA manipulation which resulted in half animal, half human creations. The myths are quite real. So this stone will aid us in forgiving our involvement in those creations.

**ENERGY LEVEL:**

# IOLITE

**CRYSTAL DESCRIPTION:** Iolite can be grey, blue to violet, yellow to brown, greenish and even clear. It can be found in metamorphic and igneous rocks, and in magmatites as a by-product of volcanic action. It can be transparent to translucent.

**USES:** Iolite or Cordierite is an attuning stone for the coming things that man will hear and see and sense that are beyond his understanding at this point. Many of the stones discovered by different entities and named different things are still the same. Because a name gives a little different frequency, a little different energy, a little different response pattern, depending on what it is called would modify the subtleties and how it would make the changes. Iolite connects with some of the most ancient places in the islands of Hawaii which are so associated with a lot of the very deep mysteries. So, that frequency is actually higher and again, it depends on what the person is feeling into and even where they are as to what they would call it and what they would resonate to.

**ANECDOTE:** Iolite at one time was touted as a less expensive gemstone to replace Sapphire. It was even called water Sapphire. Cut and polished, it is a beautiful gemstone.

**ENERGY LEVEL:** ▯

# JADE

**CRYSTAL DESCRIPTION:** Jade is typically green but can occur in white, blue, grey, mauve and, if iron oxide is present, yellow and brown. Jade is translucent and is found in serpentinized ultra-basic igneous rocks and in some schists.

**USES:** In general, Jade is a healing stone. Tranquility is a great part of its nature. The colors work in slightly different ways. Blue Jade is a throat soother for those who are having a great deal of difficulty speaking up and for those who fear public speaking. It may also be used for those who experience hoarseness and loss of the voice in tense situations. This simply relaxes the will. Green Jade aids digestion and is warmer than Turquoise. Turquoise comes and heals intensely and deeply in an emergency. Jade says, "Now that you are treated, I will hold you while you mend." The lavender Jade is especially assistive in these times for bringing in the Christ energy. It will work very well in the area of the thymus chakra. This stone loves to work with Malachite and draws on its healing energies. The Malachite works in this way as an amplifier.

**ANECDOTE:** I love working with the colors of Jade. It is so healing. In ancient China, the people would crush Jade, add it to water and drink it. That should have taken care of any digestive issues! When I noticed Malachite and lavender Jade together, I was amazed at the burst of energy that happened. It was almost like the stones embraced.

**ENERGY LEVEL:** ⬙

# JASPER

**CRYSTAL DESCRIPTION:** Jasper is a variety of Chalcedony. It has many different colors and patterns. It forms in cavities of all types of rocks, especially lava.

**USES:** Jasper is going beyond description, beyond where it has been. Jasper is changing its form in the revelation. It facilitates integrated healing on all levels. It will draw forth, to be addressed in clarity, that which the body demonstrates as out of alignment on the unseen. This assists in the understanding and achievement of balance on the unseen levels by healing dis-ease in the physical. The different colors are associated with different organs of the body. All the colors of Jasper are very high frequency and high energy stones that have been subdued and they are beginning to re-emerge into the essence and energy that was theirs.

**ANECDOTE:** Poppy Jasper is a form of wisdom of the life force. Do not fear what you create. Understand it. It helps to blend the wisdom of the heart with the kundalini life force and brings wisdom into places of denial. The yellow Jasper would be very assistive in helping humanity be in love with the fact that they are human. The Jaspers can do so much more so please explore these wonderful stones further.

**ENERGY LEVEL:** ⬧ ⬧

# KUNZITE

**CRYSTAL DESCRIPTION:** As with the Hiddenite, Kunzite is a variety of Spodumene and can be white, colorless and pink or lavender. The colors within it shift.

**USES:** Kunzite is one of the heart stones and instills self-love and is strong enough to break the emotional blocks that make one susceptible to diseases such as aids.

**ANECDOTE:** Kunzite is one of the trilogy of heart stones. This consists of Rose Quartz, Kunzite and pink Tourmaline. One by one, these crystals will break open the heart so that one might recognize the love there.

**ENERGY LEVEL:**

# KYANITE-BLUE

**CRYSTAL DESCRIPTION:** Kyanite also occurs in other colors such as white, grey, green, yellow, pink, orange or almost black. This silicate crystal can be transparent to translucent. It is found in many of the metamorphic rocks.

**USES:** Blue Kyanite is a crystal of star frequency, a higher vibration of Lapis that goes beyond the physical into the stars. It will open the heart and inform it. When used with Tourmaline, the heart will be informed of the Christ energy. This could also be used on either side of the ears for balance.

**ANECDOTE:** When working with blue Kyanite, I often find that I'm lead to use it above the head. It's like a bridge from the physical energy to star energy.

**ENERGY LEVEL:**

# KYANITE-GREEN

**CRYSTAL DESCRIPTION:** Green Kyanite can be very green or form in a combination with the blue in blades.

**USES:** Green Kyanite is about opening soul to heart to throat so that the truth is spoken through the heart but without the ego's filtering of romance or it has got to be the right thing or it has to be sweet. It is about allowing truth to be spoken forth in compassionate objectivity rather than doing the right thing. This is calling forth for the understanding of truth to be spoken without the emotions of the heart getting in the way. This is truly a filter of 'what will they say.'

**ANECDOTE:** When I first saw green Kyanite, I loved it immediately. And then, when I discovered the deep emerald green color, I couldn't believe my eyes. All Kyanite is beautiful but I am so drawn to the green stones. Maybe, just maybe, it's because green is the color of healing!

**ENERGY LEVEL:** ⬦

# KYANITE-ORANGE

**CRYSTAL DESCRIPTION:** Orange Kyanite forms in rough blades.

**USES:** Orange Kyanite is bringing in some of the energy and the essence of Bustamite and some of the energy and essence of Mahogany Obsidian. So there is a grounding while really bringing the recognition of what the thymus chakra stands for and how pertinent that Christ Consciousness is in these times. When placed in different areas on the body, it has a different kind of activation of spiritual energy. I have always felt that these require to be used in pairs.

**ANECDOTE:** Orange Kyanite is a relatively new discovery. I feel it has a very high frequency when used in pairs.

**ENERGY LEVEL:** ⬦ ⬦ ⬦

# LABRADORITE

**CRYSTAL DESCRIPTION:** Labradorite is a feldspar which exhibits chatoyancy. The colors vary and can be blue, grey, white or colorless. It rarely forms in crystals but primarily massive formations. Labradorite is an important part of certain igneous and metamorphic rocks.

**USES:** Labradorite will assist in cutting the cords of bondage of those who would be involved in the egotistical aspects of war, peacemaking if you will, but also laying to rest warlike issues. It will clear great amounts of energy from the solar plexus and the throat.

**ANECDOTE:** A lot of the Labradorite we see comes from Canada and is usually vibrant colored blues and greys. When I see this stone and it comes from Madagascar, it is called Spectrolite and usually has green, yellow and red colors as well as the blue.

**ENERGY LEVEL:**

# LAPIS LAZULI

**CRYSTAL DESCRIPTION:** Lapis is a dark blue variety of Lazurite. It usually forms in limestones metamorphosed by heat. The Lapis from Afghanistan is high quality and most contains grains of pyrite. It is found in many places, including the US and Canada as well as the eastern bloc countries.

**USES:** Lapis carries the highest vibration possible in the physical. It allows mental calming while promoting spiritual growth. Forever Lord Michael's stone, it's drawing in more and more of the grandeur of his frequency. The pink that is becoming more and more associated with the third eye is not necessarily to obscure or over-ride the color or energy of Lapis nearly so much as it is to simply blend with it as though one would draw a cloak about them, a pink mantle. But basically, what they are about is the very dark blue, deep, connected to outer space, vast.

**ANECDOTE:** I find I use this stone frequently in layouts. Its healing power is enormous. For those opting for holistic options in their care, it may help to alleviate the symptoms of advanced stages of lung dis-ease.

**ENERGY LEVEL:**

# LARIMAR

**CRYSTAL DESCRIPTION:** Larimar is a rare variety of the silicate mineral Pectolite. The only place it has been found is in the Dominican Republic in the Caribbean. Sometimes, it has a red mineral running through it but is usually an amazing blue.

**USES:** Larimar is an aspect of the coming times. We are told that it was teleported here from another planet where it was liquid. The planet of origin is of a love vibration beyond pink, an unconditional love that man would find nauseating, cloying, because unconditional love will not leave you alone, it surrounds you, it is a part of you, it has no barriers, separation or distinctions. For flexibility and tranquility, it works well with Lepidolite. On the throat, it gentles the will. For those who are very angry, very determined to force their words, it gentles the words.

**ANECDOTE:** From the time I discovered this stone, I've liked being around it. My sister-in-law was experiencing strong neck pain. The night she told me about it, I had a dream where I was told to use the Larimar on her neck for flexibility. It really helped but truly, we have to discover emotionally the cause of the creation. Maybe a 'stiff-necked attitude?' I do pay attention to the old sayings.

**ENERGY LEVEL:**

# LEPIDOLITE

**CRYSTAL DESCRIPTION:** Lepidolite forms in massive ways. It is often associated with pink Tourmaline. A more crystalline occurrence forms with Mica and Quartz. It contains lithium and can be found in veins rich in tin.

**USES:** One of many of my favorite stones, Lepidolite is a natural tranquilizer due to the lithium. It is an excellent stone for dealing with stress, PMS, hyperactivity and even aids those who are experiencing seizures. One may carry the stone, create an elixir to drink or bathe with it. Over time, the effect will build up.

**ANECDOTE:** My friends laugh when I call stones my favorite. They tell me I never met a stone I didn't like! That might be true. Lepidolite, though, is an excellent stone to add to your collection. When it contains the pink Tourmaline, it helps to support the heart.

**ENERGY LEVEL:**

# MALACHITE

**CRYSTAL DESCRIPTION:** Malachite is a rich green carbonate. Common forms are stalactites, masses with a fibrous, banded structure and crusts. It is translucent to opaque. It often forms with Azurite. It is found in the oxidized regions of copper deposits. The fibrous form has a silky luster.

**USES:** Malachite is a marvelous all-around healing stone for the whole body. Used in most layouts, it has the ability to absorb pain, both mental and physical. The tumbled stones placed on the site of physical discomfort can really bring a healing. The fibrous or crystalline form in its wildness, because it hasn't been placed in restraint or confinement by the hand of man, works in releasing the source of the pain and allowing it to leave. The tumbled Malachite will draw the pain into it and require to be cleansed. The wild state expresses it out much like the Carborundum and doesn't need to be cleansed.

**ANECDOTE:** When we are letting go of old emotions, sometimes there is a resistance which can cause physical pain. I have experienced this and can vouch for a real pain. That is where Malachite is so helpful. It can quickly relieve the pain.

**ENERGY LEVEL:**

# MERLINITE

**CRYSTAL DESCRIPTION:** Merlinite, with the technical name of Psilomelane, is black, brownish black and grey and is opaque. It can occur with Calcite which gives it a crystal look. It forms in Manganese deposits.

**USES:** Merlinite is for remembering magik with a K. For those who are delving deep into their Plutonium depths, this assists in opening the void. This is how Merlin is stepping forth from his cave in these times to assist humanity to remember the magik and so, for all of those aspiring to the magik, the Merlinite is an imperative.

**ANECDOTE:** Magik with a K is the ancient magik, not the illusions we associate with magic. Years ago, one of my friends called me from Florida and told me she had found this magical crystal. I told her to go ahead and buy it for me. The piece I have has the Calcite but also has microscopic crystals that make the stone feel like velvet. If I would touch it very hard, it would crush those tiny crystals. It truly is magikal!

**ENERGY LEVEL:** ⧰ ⧰

# MOLDAVITE

**CRYSTAL DESCRIPTION:** Moldavite forms as a result of meteors colliding with the earth. It is the only known green tektite.

**USES:** Moldavite is called dynamite in a small package. It deals with heart energy, life energy and the breaking up of major blocks in those areas. When one is in intense fear, in denial of love, the result is intense blockage to one's prosperity and creativity. Moldavite breaks free the flow of energy so where it was dammed, it will go forth.

**ANECDOTE:** Moldavite is very powerful and has a unique energy. Useful, too!

**ENERGY LEVEL:**

# MOONSTONE

**CRYSTAL DESCRIPTION:** Moonstone is an Orthoclase Feldspar and occurs in a number of colors. Most Moonstone has shifting light in it. White or cream seems to be the most recognizable. Rainbow Moonstone has mostly blue colors that shift within it.

**USES:** The white color has always been an aspect of the purity of the Goddess, an aspect of the inner nature, the feminine self and how to receive. It allows the love of the feminine nature, the Goddess. Many will have a great fear of it, being attracted and repelled as by a cobra, for they desire the powerful love of the Goddess and fear their abuse of it in other times. If you would capture the essence of Isis, the magik, the essential nature in the heart, that energy of beloved mother when the entity desires to be held, the Rainbow Moonstone would assist. It is the essence of the divine Goddess to assist the woman within to know her power.

**ANECDOTE:** Moonstone is a very popular stone and a lot can be done with it. It makes beautiful jewelry and is a good way to be in the energy.

**ENERGY LEVEL:**

# MUSCOVITE

‹⁓⁓⁓⁓⁓⁓⁓⁓⁓⁓⁓⁓⁓⁓⁓⁓⁓⁓⁓⁓⁓⁓⁓⁓⁓⁓⁓›

**CRYSTAL DESCRIPTION:** Muscovite is another of the silicates and forms as compact masses and disseminated flakes. The usual colors are colorless, white and grey. These colors are often tinted with yellow, green, brown, red and violet. You can find Muscovite in igneous rocks, especially those of acid composition like granite and in metamorphic rocks such as schist and gneiss.

**USES:** In our times, man would eat pills, he would plan the diet, he would seek exercise programs to energize the body. Lavender Muscovite is natural energy. It is not harsh but a gentle acceleration of the energy to match what is required at the moment so there is not a grand burst of energy and burnout. As it is required, there is enough, enough, enough. Yellow Muscovite motivates the activity of being. The activity of being is movement of energy, very powerful but very subtle. It is decisive and quite clear, not muddled by the fear or the push of the ego. It assists the energy of the root to be pulled to the truth center so the clarity of the God-voice might be heard more readily. Divine activity.

**ANECDOTE:** These stones seem to be ideal for the times we find ourselves in. Who couldn't use more energy and clarity?

**ENERGY LEVEL:**

# OBSIDIAN

**CRYSTAL DESCRIPTION:** Obsidian is a volcanic glass formed anywhere there is volcanic activity. It comes from rapidly cooling viscous acid lava. It can occur in various colors depending on what minerals are present but the most common colors are black, mahogany and snowflake.

**USES:** Obsidian helps to dispel illusion and helps you to know you. Black Obsidian grounds and rips away illusions. When combined with the snowflake and mahogany, the process is gentled some. It is no less powerful, perhaps more so, and no less thorough despite its gentleness. The gentleness would be for those who would find black Obsidian nauseating or upsetting to their balance. Rainbow Obsidian is for those who might be especially invested in escaping themselves. This helps to draw them to center but it also pulls the wisdom of the rainbow so they can truly recognize their journey on the rainbow bridge. If they are casting their emotions about, if they are casting their minds and thoughts about, anywhere but the bridge, this will begin to line them up with the rainbow bridge.

**ANECDOTE:** I feel we all have our favorite illusions about a lot of things. Illusion is about denying what the truth is, what is really real. It really pays to know who we are in the scheme of things.

**ENERGY LEVEL:**

# ONYX

~~~~~~~~~~~~~~~~~~~~~~~~~~~~~~~~~~~~~~~~~~~~~~~~~~~~~~~~~~~~~~~~~~~~~~~

**CRYSTAL DESCRIPTION:** Onyx is Chalcedony which is a microcrystalline form of Quartz. This occurs in many colors and can be found in cavities in rocks of different types, especially lava.

**USES:** Black Onyx is very grounding when the energy is attempting to leave the body or when one is running away, uncentered or scattered. All Onyx grounds to a greater or lesser extent, depending on the color. The lighter colors work more essentially than the black which is more physical. For holding self to Self, black is much more cohesive.

**ANECDOTE:** There are times when someone comes to me for assistance in healing and when we begin the layout, they simply leave their body, not wanting to deal with what might come up. Of course, you have to stay present to participate in your own healing. The black Onyx keeps them in their body!

**ENERGY LEVEL:** ⬡

# OPAL

**CRYSTAL DESCRIPTION:** Opal has many different colors and shapes. Precious Opal is milky white or black, with a brilliant interplay of colors, commonly red, blue and yellow. The colors often change due to the warming of water in the mineral. Fire Opal is orange or reddish and may or may not have an interplay of colors. Common Opal can be many colors and has no play of colors. Opal is transparent to opaque. This usually forms at low temperatures in silica-rich water, especially around hot springs, but can occur in almost any geological environment.

**USES:** Fire Opals are sometimes called Jelly Opals and are like volcanic energy. They come from the core of the earth and the seat of the void, from the soul of the root chakra. In these times, there is the celebration of the Goddess emerging. This particular energy assists those who are in rage to release energies from the fires of the womb. It also assists in releasing the will. Precious Opals alter moods, working with moon energy, nearly like Moonstone. Andean pink and blue Opals are common Opals from Peru. The blue is left-brained and the pink is right-brained. Use these together for balance unless someone is very unbalanced on one side or the other.

**ANECDOTE:** I am pulled by the energy of all of the Opals. It is my birthstone and I've always responded to the warmth and love of it. For those coming more and more into the balance of God-Goddess-All-That-Is, this precious stone is worth discovering.

**ENERGY LEVEL:**

# PEACOCK ORE

**CRYSTAL DESCRIPTION:** Peacock Ore is Chalcopyrite that in a lot of cases has been treated with acid to produce a strongly-colored iridescent color. This does, however, occur naturally in nature. This is a copper mineral.

**USES:** Peacock Ore assists in removing toxins from the body. When used with Rose Quartz, it acts almost as an antibiotic. It is particularly useful in areas of intense pain with help from Quartz and Malachite. This creates a balancing of healing attention to infection that lifts and moves toxins so the body may release them more readily. This also works somewhat as a blood purifier. The higher blue and violet colors are more calming, but if someone is languid or comatose, use the brighter oranges, reds and golds.

**ANECDOTE:** As all of us have experienced some level of pain in our life, Peacock Ore is certainly a stone to seek out for the assistance with that.

**ENERGY LEVEL:**

# PERIDOT

**CRYSTAL DESCRIPTION:** Peridot, also known as Olivine, is a silicate. Forsteritic Olivine in a green color is known as Peridot, a gemstone. It can be transparent to translucent. It forms in basic and ultra-basic igneous rocks. It is rich in magnesium.

**USES:** Peridot is associated with Master Kuthumi and unconditional love. It bonds will, truth and unconditional love. The Forsterite, which is more crystalline in its shape, represents a higher frequency of the Peridot. It says, 'bring me a higher love, help me to attune to the higher frequencies, assist me to understand who I really am.'

**ANECDOTE:** I knew that Forsterite was a gemstone quality of Peridot because it was labeled, but it still surprised me to find the crystal forms. Master Kuthumi is an ascended Master who represents unconditional love.

**ENERGY LEVEL:**

# PRASIOLITE

**CRYSTAL DESCRIPTION:** Prasiolite is Quartz and is sometimes known as green Amethyst. It can appear to be transparent to translucent.

**USES:** Prasiolite assists in opening the throat and allowing messages of a higher understanding to be brought through in a clear way. It would not be that some other language that no one could understand would be spoken but that higher messages would become translated more easily into a verbiage that everyone could understand. The gemstone variety of Prasiolite can be so assistive in the process of allowing the intellect to connect to that spiritual depth within self. It is the element and the energy of green that can open and soothe the heart by the very clarity of the stone and the nature of its frequency. This allows the opening so that the blending of mind and soul can be so much easier. It doesn't bring enlightenment as much as It brings a sharp, clear connection so that the transmissions come through in a very clear way. No doubt.

**ANECDOTE:** The gemmy Prasiolite is a very pale and very clear crystal. You have to feel the energy of this. It is amazing.

**ENERGY LEVEL:** ⬙ ⬙ ⬙

# PREHNITE

**CRYSTAL DESCRIPTION:** Prehnite is a silicate and is found in many places across the world. In the US, it is found in Michigan and New Jersey. It is usually green in color but may be found in white, colorless, yellow or grey. It is transparent to translucent. It forms in cavities in basaltic lava.

**USES:** Prehnite is like trying to hold onto air. Its energy shifts. It holds the frequency of the runic cross, the Christed One, and the avatars that have come to assist this planet from time to time. The frequency essence is of the Ascended Masters' places. It brings, to those who can bear it, an ability to allow the higher frequencies that are coming in to penetrate them. Place on the throat that the will might be eased, that control might be surrendered. Place on the brow to allow vision from the higher energies. Prehnite transmutes and purifies as it raises the frequency and refines to the purest form. Believable, trustable, touchable. Name a judgment. Speak through it. Consider the judgment again. Forgive it. It is done. This assists in the releasing of ancient law.

**ANECDOTE:** We are coming into the times when we are accessing more and more increased frequencies. The stones that provide those frequencies are sometimes beyond what we can tolerate but when we are ready, they are there.

**ENERGY LEVEL:** ⬖ ⬖ ⬖

# PYRITE

~~~~~~~~~~~~~~~~~~~~~~~~~~~~~~~~~~~~~~~~~~~~~~~~~~~~~~~~~~~

**CRYSTAL DESCRIPTION:** Pyrite forms as cubic, pyritohedral, or octahedral crystals. The faces are often striated. The pale-yellow color gives rise to its nickname, 'fools gold.' It is opaque with a metallic luster. Pyrite is a common assessor mineral in igneous, sedimentary and metamorphic rocks. Fine crystals occur in hydrothermal veins.

**USES:** Pyrite is an excellent grounding stone. You could call this a stone that would separate the wheat from the chaff, that type of filtering process that would allow you to define what we would call the spiritual gifts or higher levels of awareness from trivia or intellectual trash. This works as a definitive tool of clarifying the difference where judgment has taken over and blurred the edges and caused a distortion that makes the entities angry with themselves or fearful of their creations or judgmental of other people or things in their lives. And so, it really does help to some extent to transmute judgment.

**ANECDOTE:** Years ago, I was given a way to cleanse the crystals and stones and recharge them rapidly. This is gentler than using salt or salt water. I have small pieces of Pyrite that are added to pure water and after washing each stone under warm water, I swish them in the Pyrite water to finish the cleansing and recharging.

**ENERGY LEVEL:**

~~~~~~~~~~~~~~~~~~~~~~~~~~~~~~~~~~~~~~~~~~~~~~~~~~~~~~~~~~~

# QUARTZ-BLUE

**CRYSTAL DESCRIPTION:** There are many colors of Quartz and most carry the Quartz name.

**USES:** The essence of Blue Quartz is similar but more grounded than that of Celestite. It is more of the earth. Celestite calls the essence of the stars while this would be like feet on the ground and head in the stars. It brings tranquility and soothes the disturbed spirit. There is a lot of disturbance in the spirit waters now because of the conflicts in the healing of the separation and so much of what has been called 'right' must be forgiven. In God, those things have no place. There is no right or wrong so this will assist those who have disturbed spirit to walk more peacefully their own path and not be in so much conflict when they find others are not in agreement with what they are becoming.

**ANECDOTE:** There is so much conflict on this earth that anything that can help us to stay grounded and help heal that conflict is something we really require to explore.

**ENERGY LEVEL:** 🔹 🔹

# QUARTZ-GOLDEN HEALING

**CRYSTAL DESCRIPTION:** Golden Healing Quartz is mined in Arkansas. It is not plentiful but can be found. The color is probably from an exposure in Iron.

**USES:** There are things we are bringing into the earth, to be found in these times, that man has known to exist before. Golden Healing Quartz carries the properties of the essences, of thoughts, of herbs, considerations of healing that were called to crystallized form and brought forth in this time from Lemuria, from Atlantis, from all places of great healing through the ages of this earth. Now it is put in a physical form to be accessed. It may be placed upon the body for healing in specific areas but especially for the truth in the solar plexus.

**ANECDOTE:** In ancient times, the wands were of very clear Quartz wrapped in pure gold. This is the essence of the two brought together. It is exhilarating to work with.

**ENERGY LEVEL:**

# QUARTZ-PHANTOM

**CRYSTAL DESCRIPTION:** Phantom Quartz have the outline of another point within them. There are a number of different colors and minerals that form the phantom.

**USES:** All of the Phantom Quartz clear illusions, relieving trapped mind patterns and riders in the aura. The white Phantom would be more for balancing. The red Phantom is more for those who have no ambition, whether mental, physical, emotional or spiritual. It is a motivator. The green Phantom is particularly helpful in balancing the red tones of a virus. It may aid those with cancer of the lymph system. It is extremely healing.

**ANECDOTE:** While I never recommend someone not seek medical help, we have tools to make their lives easier as well as balance the energy so whatever health method they choose will work optimally.

**ENERGY LEVEL:**

# QUARTZ-ROSE

**CRYSTAL DESCRIPTION:** As the name suggests, the Rose Quartz is a pink form of Quartz. It rarely forms as a crystal and more in massive deposits. Large deposits have been discovered in South Dakota.

**USES:** Rose Quartz is the color of love. It is a gentle energy that helps one to love self and others. It opens the heart to allow the love to come in. Even though the color of the heart chakra is green, Rose Quartz has been used extensively in the heart area.

**ANECDOTE:** Rose Quartz is part of the love trinity. It is the first stone used in the process to assist the heart to open.

**ENERGY LEVEL:**

# QUARTZ-RUTILATED

**CRYSTAL DESCRIPTION:** Rutilated Quartz is clear Quartz that has strands of other minerals running through it. Those strands can be several different colors and are minerals that were present when the Quartz was forming.

**USES:** The Rutiles are much like filaments of information. They are messages encoded in the stones. It is electrical, electronic as the psyche soars, as the entity allows oneself to be less limited by the old ways. The electricity, the electronics, the computerization of Rutilated Quartz will be decoded. There are messages in the crystal that as the entity raises their vibrational frequency, they will be able to decode the message. A lot of the messages will be similar to those found on the Wing Makers site online: how magnificent you are, how wonderful you are, how grand you are, how far beyond what you believe you are. This is technology that would exceed the comprehension of the finite mind of man.

**ANECDOTE:** The appearance of these crystals is striking. I have an obelisk that has red Rutiles in it. In the sun, it is stunning. I saw a sphere of Rutilated Quartz that I coveted. Unfortunately, it belonged to someone else! It had been cut in such a way that the golden Rutiles came to the surface of the sphere. It looked like a ball of stars.

**ENERGY LEVEL:**

# QUARTZ-SKELETAL

**CRYSTAL DESCRIPTION:** Skeletal Quartz is so named because of its structure. You can see through all the levels of the crystal. The majority is light to dark Smoky Quartz. Sometimes, it forms with Tourmaline.

**USES:** At this point in time, those who are looking back might get something out of this but it hasn't come into its time yet for those who are looking forward. Those who are looking back would associate it with dinosaurs and something that is very old. Those who are looking forward would begin to connect with the ancient wisdom and not just the old. There are very few who would understand what this is about yet.

**ANECDOTE:** The structure of this is fascinating. A person could get lost in the nooks and crannies of this.

**ENERGY LEVEL:**

# QUARTZ-SMOKY

**CRYSTAL DESCRIPTION:** The smoky color of the Smoky Quartz is caused by the presence of radiation in the earth. The color ranges from light to dark brown and is usually transparent.

**USES:** One of the grounding stones, this brings the white light down through the body to the base of the spine and grounds it there. It would also aid in cleansing the body. In these times, this crystal helps to define mystery from darkness. There are those who are afraid of the dark and therefore cannot access the mysteries because they are so afraid. Smoky Quartz would be very helpful placed on the third eye or the solar plexus and, for some, even in the root chakra. This helps them to journey into themselves and it works almost like the light on a miner's helmet so they can see more clearly into their own darkness and the treasures that are there. The revelation of the mysteries.

**ANECDOTE:** One year when I was in Tucson for a large gem and mineral show, I walked into a showroom filled with Smoky Quartz. The crystals I was looking at had been bombarded with radiation in a lab. It was beautiful and a deep, almost black but it was screaming. That is the only way I can describe it. I had to leave that room and quickly. I really attempt to steer clear of the stones that have been dyed, stabilized or irradiated. I feel it isn't something I would like to use in the healing room.

**ENERGY LEVEL:**

# QUARTZ-SPIRIT

〜〜〜〜〜〜〜〜〜〜〜〜〜〜〜〜〜〜〜〜〜〜〜〜〜〜〜〜

**CRYSTAL DESCRIPTION:** This Quartz forms in such a way that the crystals are tiny. This occurs in Amethyst, White Quartz and Yellow Quartz.

**USES:** Spirit Quartz in these times is especially amazing for stepping through the veil between human and fairy realms and to work with the fairies and to connect with them, for it has been a bit of a joke to humanity that all fairies are a bit like Tinker Bell. And yet, the fairy realm has a great influence on the human realms especially in working with the magik. The fairies carry a lot of the remembering of how the magik works, which humanity really requires in these times. And so, these connect with the fairy realms.

**ANECDOTE:** The one time I explored the fairy realms, I was quite surprised. Tinker Bell they're not! There are many who don't believe in humans just as there are those humans who don't believe in fairies. When the fairies closed the portals between our realm and theirs, it was because they didn't want their realm to experience what had happened to the earth. There are still those fairies that are angry because of what we've done to the earth. But there are others who want to repair the rifts between them and us.

**ENERGY LEVEL:**

〜〜〜〜〜〜〜〜〜〜〜〜〜〜〜〜〜〜〜〜〜〜〜〜〜〜〜〜

# RHODOCHROSITE

**CRYSTAL DESCRIPTION:** Rhodochrosite commonly forms in massive formations but can occur in crystalline shapes. The color is typically pink to red but can demonstrate brown, yellowish or orange hues. It is transparent to translucent. This forms in hydrothermal veins and in altered manganese deposits.

**USES:** Rhodochrosite is powerful and will break up blocks in the entire body. It also helps to break addictions and compulsions. Ideally, pair with Variscite. The crystal form is another way, a different path of bringing in higher love. As the love truly permeates and integrates, the judgments that have brought conflict and addiction begin to simply melt away. Therefore, the compulsions and addictions that have been so inspired by fear almost feel like they have been withdrawn and there is no necessity to do anything about them. Just let them go. This assists not only in the overcoming but in the fulfilling release of addictive-compulsive behavior.

**ANECDOTE:** When paired with Variscite, Rhodochrosite begins to break the addictions and the Variscite will bring in the understanding of why the addiction is there in the first place.

**ENERGY LEVEL:**

# RHODONITE

**CRYSTAL DESCRIPTION:** Rhodonite forms as tabular crystals, usually with rounded edges, and massive, compact and granular habits. Its color is pink to rose-red or brownish-red. It often has black veins of manganese-rich altered sediments. This forms in metamorphic rocks rich in manganese.

**USES:** Rhodonite assists those who would go to find their own internal darkness to not be afraid of what is there. It is a balancing, harmonizing stone. For one who is extremely righteous, it would be well for them to carry it at all times.

**ANECDOTE:** Sometimes, it is a challenge to tell the difference between Rhodochrosite and Rhodonite as they are often the same colors. Usually you can do this by looking for the black veins in Rhodonite. The Rhodochrosite usually has more white in it.

**ENERGY LEVEL:**

# RUBY

**CRYSTAL DESCRIPTION:** A variety of Corundum, Ruby is red. It is translucent to transparent and it can be found in rocks. Because of its hardness and density, it may also be found in river gravels.

**USES:** A stronger vibration of Garnet, this helps to raise the kundalini energy. The Ruby, as with Emerald, is definitely a heart stone. It stands halfway between the red of the root chakra and the purple of the crown. That makes this a marvelous access stone to the royalty of self. It is about defining our divine nature and feeling more comfortable with our own divinity. This transmutes the energies of 'I'm not really that good. I don't really deserve that much, I'm not really that worthy, I don't accomplish that magnificently.' This transmutes those judgments and brings a recognition, a realization.

**ANECDOTE:** Ruby works well with pink Tourmaline in the heart area because of the transmuting energy to help us recognize, in love, who we truly are.

**ENERGY LEVEL:** ▯

# RUBY STEMS

**CRYSTAL DESCRIPTION:** Ruby Stems are a natural formation of Ruby.

**USES:** The formation of Ruby Stems has a certain healing ability. This does not necessarily heal a virus but it greatly assists as a computer directed force that would assist the antibodies within the physical vehicle to properly recognize and identify what they are dealing with. There are times when things are mislabeled or misdiagnosed when we are having challenges, creating stress in the body. The Ruby Stems assist the body to say, 'Here is a foreign matter, here is a poison, here is a toxin, here is a disease maker. This crystal assists the body to find an appropriate way to deal with it. This would also act as a blood purifier.

**ANECDOTE:** Can you imagine a crystal that would help you to discover just what is going on with your body? I find that amazing.

**ENERGY LEVEL:** ⬙

# SAPPHIRE

~~~~~~~~~~~~~~~~~~~~~~~~~~~~~~~~~~~~~~~~~~~~~~~~~~~~~~~~~~

**CRYSTAL DESCRIPTION:** Sapphire is the blue variety of Corundum. While blue is the most common color, it can also occur in green, yellow, purple or colorless. It is transparent to translucent and forms in certain igneous and metamorphic rocks.

**USES:** Sapphire will assist in opening both the throat and the third eye chakras. Use with Quartz for amplification of the essences. As with many of the rare stones and gemstones, its energy is very high. The Quartz amplifies the essence and intensifies treatment. Use wisely. There are those who could not bear it. If each one would recognize what is coming to you through your crown chakra, your cranial cavity, it isn't just your physical brain but the resonance of the pineal and pituitary and all of the connectors electrically. It is the energy, the power that is coming in, the crystal skull, the headdress of the pharaoh, all significant indicators that something is coming to the mind from a higher consciousness and that it requires some kind of a funnel. The Sapphire will provide that energetic funnel.

**ANECDOTE:** Before I met my future husband, I had no idea that some Sapphires were colorless. He had a collection of those. I found out that when you take colorless Sapphire and heat it to a high heat it turns an amazing blue! And then I began to see other colors. Mother Nature is quite wonderful.

**ENERGY LEVEL:** ◊ ◊ ◊

~~~~~~~~~~~~~~~~~~~~~~~~~~~~~~~~~~~~~~~~~~~~~~~~~~~~~~~~~~

# SELENITE

---

**CRYSTAL DESCRIPTION:** Selenite is a sulfate and occurs in many shapes and colors such as white, colorless, grey, greenish, yellowish, brownish, reddish and orange. It is transparent to opaque.

**USES:** Selenite provides essential healing for emotions of the higher level of nature as a bridge into feelings. It assists in gentling the chaos of the egotistical nature. It aligns things so they flow more freely into the feeling nature. Pieces create a vortex. Wands are directional and move energy away from the body. Orange Selenite works a little differently. Because the spleen chakra is so involved with owning one's power and bringing the emotions on line so that they serve you rather than depress you or bring you low, this is an excellent stone for the entity to sit with at navel level for reconnecting with power, calling power home, meshing all of the energies that have been given for lifetimes, bringing emotion to center so there is a sense of peace and joy in the emotional nature rather than conflict and fear. This is very much like a love lotion to the chaos and wounding that has occurred around the second chakra.

**ANECDOTE:** There is an abundance of shapes of Selenite. We have Selenite roses, triangles, small flat blades and even a form called Duck-Billed Selenite that demonstrates crystals that look like a duck bill. Some people use Selenite to charge crystals. It has so many uses.

**ENERGY LEVEL:**

# SERAFINITE

**CRYSTAL DESCRIPTION:** Serafinite is a variety of Clinochlore. It may be white to yellowish or colorless as well as green. It is transparent to opaque with a pearly luster.

**USES:** Serafinite is a little piece of the universe brought in for remembering. If you would take the flowers and the jewels and compress the essential understanding into a solid place, you would have a memory of those things given to the earth for man's healing before he ever came here. It reawakens cellular memory and assists in the forgiveness of blocks. At this point, this would not be used on the body.

**ANECDOTE:** Serafinite is just a reminder that humanity has been given many tools for healing our challenges. It certainly is a beautiful stone with its silvery swirls in the dark green. This stone is sometimes spelled Seraphinite. I've seen it both ways.

**ENERGY LEVEL:**

# SERPENTINE

**CRYSTAL DESCRIPTION:** Serpentine's colors are green, grey to black, white and brownish. It can be fibrous or solid. It is often accompanied by Chlorite, Olivine, Chromite, Magnetite, Dolomite, Talc and Quartz.

**USES:** Serpentine helps to raise the kundalini energy. A layout to facilitate that follows. This pattern would work on the front of the body as well as on the back. Place Serpentine on the root chakra and in the area of the neck with rainbow colors in between. Starting at the root, use Serpentine, Poppy Jasper, Carnelian, Citrine, Chrysoprase, Kunzite or pink Tourmaline, Lapis or Azurite, then definitely Lapis or one of the light pink stones such as Kunzite or pink Tourmaline on the third eye and Amethyst, Sugilite or even perhaps Lepidolite at the crown, for the crown is moving to the very light violet colors.

**ANECDOTE:** This layout would work for someone who is ready to make a shift in energy. This calls for a willingness to embrace the higher energies and connections.

**ENERGY LEVEL:** ⬦ ⬦

# SMITHSONITE

**CRYSTAL DESCRIPTION:** Smithsonite is a carbonate and occurs in several colors. It can be white, grey, yellow, green, blue, pink, purple and brown. It is translucent and has a pearly luster. Some have a spattering of druzy.

**USES:** Smithsonite assists the body to be comfortable and balanced as the energy accelerates. Not a generator, nor truly an amplifier, it is more a stabilizer for the very high energies currently happening. Use in the heart and groin areas at the same time.

**ANECDOTE:** Smithsonite was named for the founder of the Smithsonian Institute. As the energy becomes stronger and stronger, we sometimes experience rapid heartbeats as well as other discomforts. This can really help to alleviate those things.

**ENERGY LEVEL:** ⬘

# SODALITE

**CRYSTAL DESCRIPTION:** Sodalite is a silicate. Its primary color is blue but occurs in other colors as well. It can be white, colorless, yellowish, greenish, or reddish. It is a transparent to translucent mineral. It forms in certain igneous rocks.

**USES:** Sodalite acts as a weak antibiotic. Gentler than penicillin, it needs help and support from other stones such as white Fluorite or clear Quartz. This is a friend to the Lapis and it is very assistive in dissolving intuitive or spiritual indigestion where the emotional nature has gone into such conflict that perhaps the physical belly is responding. There is a tremendous amount in this time of poor digestion because so many entities are confronting aspects of themselves that don't set well with them. As this stone would be placed in the solar plexus and the Lapis would be placed over the third eye, the energy and information that would be bridged there would draw down higher levels of understanding and help them to be palatable, more acceptable and also more understandable. You could say it is almost like an interpreter stone that would bring higher levels of information into a more grounded or easily understood point for humanity.

**ANECDOTE:** I have used this for a sore throat. A piece of clear Quartz would enhance the healing energy.

**ENERGY LEVEL:** ⬡

# SUGILITE

CRYSTAL DESCRIPTION: Sugilite is a rare purple cyclosilicate mineral. It gets its color from traces of manganese. The most valuable Sugilite is a uniform and intense purple. The best qualities come from South Africa.

USES: Sugilite has a high frequency like Lapis only gentler. A good heart stone, this will work with the thymus chakra as well. It carries the heart to higher frequencies of understanding once the heart is open.

ANECDOTE: The purple color is important here, purple being the color of transformation. I really have to look for this stone at market. Some, I'm quite sure, is dyed, so find a reputable dealer.

ENERGY LEVEL:

# TEMPEST STONE

**CRYSTAL DESCRIPTION:** Pietersite is more commonly known as Tempest Stone. It evolved from crocidolite before being replaced by Quartz. It carries a lot of Tiger Eye. Its colors vary but it is mostly blue. It sometimes has yellow and reds within it.

**USES:** Tempest Stone brings form out of chaos in this time of exquisite ego. A cabochon may be used for clearing emotion. A wand brings the will into alignment. This stone broadcasts tranquility. Where there is conflict on earth, placing the Tempest Stone in those areas on a map can be very assistive to peacemaking. It is almost as though a small piece of this stone could be placed on each chakra all the time because it helps to bring a communication between those sources that do not communicate. If there are chakras that are shut down, withdrawn or do not act in accordance with the others, this will assist them to align when the eye is single. It also assists people who absolutely cannot conceive that anyone has anything, any thought, any concept that could possibly be as good as theirs. For those in political office that simply believe that their ideas are the only ways things can be done, placing a piece of this stone on a picture would be very helpful.

**ANECDOTE:** With all the chaos we are dealing with in the world, these ideas for ways to help are certainly something to pursue. The Masters remind us that if we heal the war within all of us, the world would heal!

**ENERGY LEVEL:**

# TIGER-EYE

**CRYSTAL DESCRIPTION:** Tiger-Eye is actually a variety of Quartz. It is golden brown, sometimes with blue. The blue is called Hawks Eye. The red Tiger-Eye is actually heated to create the red color. It is found in South Africa.

**USES:** The gold Tiger-Eye is a wisdom stone and strengthens your personal shield. It assists those who would be called magik or wizard to create an aura of invisibility or to work with the art of illusion. It is a shape-shifters stone.

**ANECDOTE:** It is so good to find stones that will help with our everyday protection. As you embrace your growing vibrations, this would help to connect you to the ancient magik.

**ENERGY LEVEL:**

# TOURMALINE

CRYSTAL DESCRIPTION: Tourmaline forms in many colors including pink, green, blue and black and combinations and most are vertically striated. It is transparent to opaque. It can be found in granites and pegmatites, as well as in some metamorphic rocks.

USES: Tourmaline balances the emotions. It is a high frequency stone that amplifies. It also is a stone of revelation and magik. It assists in understanding what would be called the mysteries of life. Tourmaline, no matter what its color, is very associated with the heart. Therefore, even the black tourmaline would open things that have been hidden, moving into the secret chambers, accessing deep spiritual connection and union.

ANECDOTE: I often use a spiral of pink and green Tourmaline in the heart area in a layout. It helps one with self-love and healing.

ENERGY LEVEL:

# TURQUOISE

**CRYSTAL DESCRIPTION:** Turquoise is bright blue to pale blue, greenish blue, green and grey. Massive forms are opaque. It can be found in aluminum-rich igneous and sedimentary rocks that have been altered, often by surface water.

**USES:** A stone of balance, Turquoise goes to the greatest depths of healing. It has an immediate affect on trauma, especially the emotional trauma of those involved in accidents. This would be the first thing to give someone who's been in an accident as its energy is soft yet intense so the person can begin to receive healing on all levels. It will stabilize energies and bring the body into understanding of why things have been created.

**ANECDOTE:** I have used Turquoise on those struggling with edema to balance fluid and further understanding. The placement on the top of the ankles is also for lymphatic and emotional balance.

**ENERGY LEVEL:**

# UNAKITE

**CRYSTAL DESCRIPTION:** Unakite is an altered Granite composed of pink Orthoclase Feldspar, green Epidote and generally colorless Quartz.

**USES:** The Unakite brings one to an understanding of one's warrior nature and how to be peaceful with it. It works a great deal with the liver bile and the balancing of the hormones of the body and the liver that is in disorder. It would work to a certain extent with digestion and elimination on a physical level. Because the liver is where most of the anger goes, this stone is excellent for dealing with that anger. When it is used in the area of the thymus chakra and the throat, it begins to alter communication from the clipped speech or the angry intonations, to a more mellow or melodious form of communication. It deals with warrior and anger in general and certainly how if affects the balances of the body.

**ANECDOTE:** My friends used to laugh and say I didn't meet a crystal I didn't like. This was the exception. The Masters reminded me to pay attention to that which I hate. I told them that was too harsh, I just didn't like it much. When they told me it was about being a peaceful warrior, I finally understood. Most of us carry great amounts of anger within us and I am no exception. I was just unwilling to look at what that meant for me.

**ENERGY LEVEL:** 〖 〗

# VARISCITE

**CRYSTAL DESCRIPTION:** Variscite is a phosphate and it is always green. It can be transparent to translucent. It forms where water, rich in phosphates, has altered aluminum-rich rocks.

**USES:** Rhodochrosite helps heal compulsions, Jade assists digestion and Turquoise is for trauma. Put it together and you have Variscite. For those who simply will not accept their truth and seek to swallow anything that comes along, compulsively and destructively, Variscite assists them to overcome compulsions. It goes beyond the alcohol or drugs and gets to the compulsion that caused the alcohol or drugs to be there. It goes to the root cause of the compulsion. For, if you would heal one of alcoholism, you would still not have necessarily touched why it was and he will find other things to put in its place. This stone deals with anything done to escape self from inability to face what one has created: alcohol, drugs, food and tobacco. It makes self easier to deal with and provides a pathway into self for those who are fleeing. Placed on the bar at home or in public, this stone will broadcast out for those with an issue with alcohol.

**ANECDOTE:** Variscite has a texture nearly like Turquoise. How wonderful to have a stone that will help us to understand our addictions.

**ENERGY LEVEL:**

# 9

# BACK LAYOUTS

*"True strength lies in submission which permits one to dedicate his life, through devotion, to something beyond himself."*

*- Henry Miller*

The higher your vibration is, the more likely it is that you can enjoy a back layout. This layout will definitely further your growth. It aids in the kundalini rising, it gets at issues at a cellular level and triggers your remembering of who you are and why you are here at this point in time. It is a wonderful step up in vibrational levels.

My teacher had admonished her students to always lay the crystals on the front of the body and never the back. She felt the potential for harm was much greater working on someone's back. Imagine my chagrin then when I began getting images and dreams of working on the spine and doing extensive back layouts. The picture I got was of a row of small crystals on either side of the spine and those working almost like a zipper closing. The Masters recommended the type of crystal to be used but those came from the Jeffrey mine that had been closed. They are called Jeffrey or solution quartz and grow under water. I remembered an ad for some of these in a magazine and went searching for it. I finally found what I was looking for and contacted the dealer. As luck would have it, the week before he had sold his remaining supply to someone else but was willing to give me his name and phone number. I called and asked if there was any way I could purchase some of the stones from him. He told me he had about one hundred and fifty of them left and gave me a great price. Things really come together when they are meant to be.

Eagerly, I waited for them to arrive and they were exquisite and so alive, so tiny yet full of energy. Now I was ready to play with them and explore my dreams. I enlisted the help of friends for practice. The first time I laid the stones, I put the small points on either side of the spine and then a wand at the base of the neck and one at the base of the spine. I was feeling pretty proud of myself and then heard a voice telling me to place another wand on the small of the back. I told my friend that I didn't expect to do that and the voice said, "Be not in expectation!" Well! I was on my way to listening for guidance.

As I mentioned earlier, I had been cautioned to not lay the crystals on the back of the body as the potential for harm was greater than putting them on the front of the body. Not knowing or remembering that this could be done safely, I was greatly disturbed to find that I was being directed to do back layouts. This would facilitate the raising of the kundalini energy. These are strong layouts and in addition to raising the kundalini they trigger a remembering and get to blocks on a cellular level. The difference between a front layout and a back layout is like the difference between an appendectomy and brain surgery. And I was led to do this!

The very first back layout was done in early 1989 before I knew this would be an important part of my work. Gladys came to me with severe back pain, which resulted in her not being able to move freely or sleep more than two or three hours a night. With the insight given me, we ascertained that she continually put things behind her so she wouldn't have to deal with them until later. Later never came. As a result, she had what I would describe as thick calluses on the buttocks and extreme physical pain. (The pain is very real even though what I "see" is etheric.) I was directed to lay stones on her below the waist and let her lay there for thirty minutes before proceeding. At the end of that time, I made ready to remove the stones when something at the base of the spine caught my attention. Imagine my surprise when I saw a white ribbon bow poised there. As I continued to watch, the bow turned into a white butterfly and flew up the length of the spine! I am still amazed at that. Looking back, I realize that the butterfly symbolized the raising of the kundalini energy and rebirth. It was truly beautiful. I talked with her a few days later and she reported she was sleeping better than she had in months. And, she's learning to deal with things as they happen.

Many things are manifested when we work with the crystals. Each person has his or her own way of dealing with the emotions that arise. Some of those reactions are very interesting.

Betty and I made contact at a psychic fair and soon after, I was invited to her lovely home to do a workshop and layouts. It was one of those weekends in November that one seldom sees in Colorado. The weather was positively balmy with clear blue skies and fresh clean air. People wore shorts and washed their cars and gloried in being outside. The memory of it carried me through the long cold Wyoming winter that was to come.

In exchange for her hospitality, I agreed to do a layout for Betty. She arm-tested for a back layout and as I talked with her, she shared the fact that she had pain under the right shoulder blade that had been there for some time. This was another example of something manifested in the energy field that affected the physical body. I helped her to recognize what she was holding emotionally and went about removing the 'spot' with a laser wand. The wound was then energetically cauterized with violet flame for healing. The next morning, Betty told me she wanted to show me something. On her back, where the crystals had been laying across her shoulders, were marks that looked like she had been sunburned. It wasn't painful, but that must have been one hot layout!

Jeff also came to me at a fair. He said that I was the reason he was there. He really wanted to work with me and I knew we had worked together in other lifetimes. The most important of these was a lifetime when he was a student of mine, learning crystal healing. He felt he was ready to try it on his own but he still had a lot to learn and I cautioned him. Being a headstrong young man, he did as he wanted and seriously injured another being. He was so sorry for what he had done that he came into this lifetime to make amends. He had studied numerous healing methods and was still attending college to learn more. He became a perennial student because he never felt ready to go out on his own. I worked with him some through layouts, one of which stands out in my mind. He was releasing a great deal of emotion. He was on his stomach and his nose started running. There was a lot of mucous and I put a wastebasket under his head. I am still amazed at the amount of mucous he released. I later understood that the sinus cavities are where we store old energy and belief systems that no longer serve us. I find we have many ways of letting go of toxins from the body. Some people vomit or get diarrhea, some sweat profusely or get runny noses!

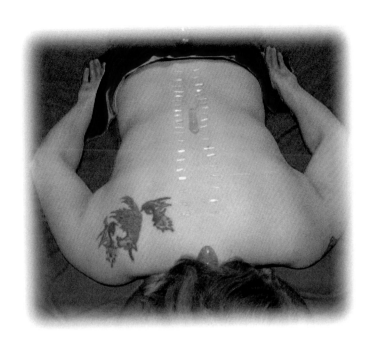

# BASIC BACK LAYOUT

**PURPOSE:** Back layouts are about beginning the process of raising the kundalini, reaching buried emotions at a cellular level and triggering a remembering of who you are and why you're here.

**USES:** In back layouts, I nearly always use the tiny Jeffrey Quartz crystals. These form under water and are a very high frequency. These line the spine which is the channel for the kundalini energy. Other crystals and stones are used to aid one to remember and process deep-seated emotions.

**ANECDOTE:** This basic back layout reflects the vision I was given for my initial back layout. I looked for the Jeffrey crystals for quite some time. The name comes from the name of the mine where they were found. I discovered that the mine had been closed but I found a man who had a supply at one time but had sold them all to someone else. He gave me the man's name and I called him. He was willing to sell me fifty of them! I was delighted when they arrived. It pays to persevere!

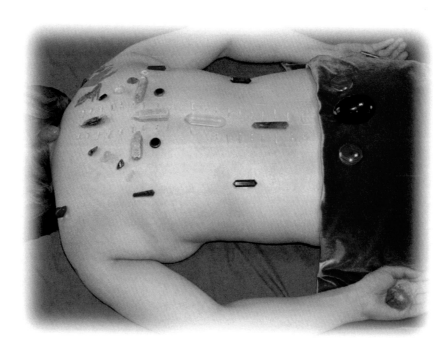

# ADVANCED BACK LAYOUT

**PURPOSE:** To reiterate, a back layout will get at things at a cellular level, begin the process of raising the kundalini and trigger the remembering.

**USES:** In this sample back layout, you will notice the Jeffrey Quartz crystals on either side of the spine. That is pretty standard in these layouts unless someone's energy has gone beyond needing that energy. The stones are placed in such a way that they are aiding the frequency of the entire body. There are a few Lepidolite with Rubellite that will create ease and healing in the heart area. The Poppy Jasper on the shoulders will also assist in the raising of the kundalini energy. The Obsidian egg on the root chakra will take one into the forgiveness of the illusions and into the void so they can begin to see who they truly are. The Malachite will take away the pain of the process when there is a resistance to letting go.

**ANECDOTE:** I have found very few who lay the stones on the back. This layout is very beneficial to take us into uncharted territory. Where we are moving to has nothing to do with where we have been. This is fearful to many of us as we don't have an inkling of what that looks like. So we leap, empty handed, into the void!

# 10

# CHAKRAS

*"It isn't down in any map. True places never are."*
- Herman Hesse

**C**hakras are those energy vortices that are present in the energy of the body as well as above and below your energy field. There are mainly 7 recognized in our body energy as well as the 13th which is at the thymus level.

Everything in life is energy and the chakras are no exception. As nothing in life is static, as we spiral upward on our journey to bodies of light, the energies, colors and many other things change. That goes for the chakras as well. You might call the chakras vortices of energy, each unique in its color and vibration. Each pertains to an element of life that requires opening and balancing. Traditionally, there are seven main chakras. There is another powerful chakra emerging in the thymus area between the heart and throat chakras. While I have done my best to supply you with up-to-date information, this is not a definitive nor comprehensive overview. The old chakra system's color energies would work with the physical plane, blending them with the spiritual integration. Spirit is moving in to embrace all of what the physical world is about. Spirit is embracing physicality, the body and physical things. It is embracing the mind and what has been called logic is beginning to be revealed as highly illogical. The old and new energies are blending. As people allow themselves to surrender to the spiritual elements, then as you are able to see the chakras, you may actually notice that some people's chakra systems are considerably lighter than others. The logical mind says they're ill, they're weak, they're sick because their chakras are lighter. The truth of it is, they're simply much more engaged in allowing the spiritual directive in their lives. They may not be aware but on a spiritual level, they have reached a point where they are willing to allow spirit to be more and more a part of their lives. They may not be intellectually conscious but they will still show a lighter chakra system. The ego mind always wants to leap on anything that it can judge about someone else even though the bible says, 'judge not, lest ye be judged.' For many metaphysical people, it is simply a pastime sitting around and denigrating other masters for not doing it, so they must be bad people. The forgiveness of judgment simply lightens the burden of everyone. The energy of judgment is heavy and it's a very difficult thing to carry. It is almost unbearable in these times. The healing and the recognition begin with the realization that as spirit moves in and integrates all of the elements of the being, then enlightenment is going to begin to show. The colors of the chakras will begin to change as we up-spiral our energy and they are infused with spirit.

## FIRST CHAKRA

As we begin our journeys on the path of enlightenment, we begin at the root chakra which is usually associated with our life force and physical experience. This chakra houses the sleeping kundalini. Current understanding says the color of this chakra is red. As our vibrations accelerate, the color of this chakra will gradually change to a deep silvery rose.

## SECOND CHAKRA

The second chakra is typically situated at navel levels. It is associated with the reproductive organs, the extension of life force beyond self and self-empowerment. We currently use the color orange for this chakra and it will turn more of a peach color with our growing vibrations.

## THIRD CHAKRA

The third chakra is located in the solar plexus area. This chakra is understood to be the truth center, the seat of the soul. This would be where we would go to dispel illusion, to find universal truth. Your gut feelings relate to this chakra and usually, if you go with that feeling, things will turn out for you. Modern use recognizes the color of yellow that will begin to be shot through with violet and purple.

## FOURTH CHAKRA

The fourth chakra is located in the heart area and is considered to be the crossroads of the chakras. Most people would associate this chakra with love as we know it and stuff all kinds of emotions pertaining to grief and heart break. But this chakra can also be about healing and forgiving self and others. It is beginning to deal with emotions before they become physical to prevent the true breaking of the heart. The color associated with the heart chakra is green, though most would think of pink as it is the color of love. This will gradually change to an emerald blue color.

## THIRTEENTH/THYMUS CHAKRA

The thirteenth chakra, the thymus, that is now opening is considered the energy of the shift in consciousness. This takes us into unconditional love, the Christ consciousness and then beyond unconditional love. What might that be like? Imagine happiness of health restored, unimaginable joy of living, ecstasy of love, freedom from fear, anger, resentment, etc. I've talked to people who have seen varying colors in this chakra but it seems to me to be like the dying embers of a campfire. That would make sense as we come to a place of 'as above, so below.' This would relate to the second chakra that is orange in color.

## FIFTH CHAKRA

The fifth chakra lies in the hollow of the throat. Its color is a dark blue that becomes more of a sky-blue. This chakra can relate to our acknowledging our truth, owning it by speaking it, if only to self. It brings us into a place of 'I will to will Thy will.'

## SIXTH CHAKRA

The sixth chakra lies on the forehead between the eyebrows. In our culture, the color is indigo or violet becoming a light violet to pink. This brings us to the point of seeing beyond what we see now and an allowance of the intuition and understanding of the various cognitive faculties of the mind.

## SEVENTH CHAKRA

The seventh chakra, or crown chakra, lies above the head. This is where kundalini ultimately connects with pure consciousness. It brings greater spiritual knowledge and is truly our connection to the Higher Self. As this occurs, the color becomes a golden white. As we near pure energy or enlightenment, the chakras become crystalline. This matches our eternal crystal structure.

# 11

# KUNDALINI

*"Remember the magik. As you stand ready to embark on a journey that always begins and never ends, remember the magik. Remember that you are not alone.*

*Never again alone."*

- Lazaris

The kundalini energy is housed in the root chakra. As we begin to become aware of the frequencies of the energies within us, the kundalini begins to awaken. This is the very beginning of the rise of energy up the spinal column and the chakras. One symbol of this rise is the Rod of Aesculapius, the ancient mythical god of medicine. This is usually depicted as a staff or rod with a snake curled around it and is the traditional sign of the medical profession. The Caduceus is often mistaken as the medical symbol but is truly the symbol of Hermes. It features two snakes winding around an often-winged staff.

Since early times, the kundalini has been a mystery to man. Most cultures had secret societies and rituals surrounding the raising of that energy. I had heard a lot about this kundalini energy and I was curious. If I was going to do the back layouts, and it looked like I was, I wanted to know more. Primarily, I wanted to know why some people experienced varying degrees of pain as the energy rose through the spine while others weren't aware of anything at all. In my communications with Lord St. Germain, I asked about this. The information given me was enlightening. The kundalini is the life force energy and connection to the God-force. When pain is experienced in the awakening of this drive, the Masters would ask, "How much God can you stand?" It is like struggling against being born. There we are, in the birth canal, hanging on for dear life, digging our heels in and experiencing great pain when we could relax and welcome our emergence into the light. With the awakening of this energy, the sexual energy is also enhanced. Some will choose to remain in a lustful state of being, rather than exploring other options because they enjoy the sexual feelings so much. There is no right or wrong in this as God, Goddess created all to be enjoyed, but if this basic, creative energy was transformed into higher energy our spiritual growth would be grand indeed.

As I began to work with this life force energy and became aware of 'seeing' it, it appeared not as a serpent but as a dragon. The dragons were all different: different sizes, colors, and movements. I've seen little 'Puff, the Magic Dragon', quite small, and huge scale rattling manifestations. Some have wings, others do not. Some are very feminine, others masculine. I am constantly amazed at the variety of colors. The first one I was ever aware of I saw during a layout on my friend, Molly. I don't recall that it was so large as exquisite. It was a brilliant white with a shiny gold trim and the head appeared to look something like a seahorse. It made its way up the body, got to the top of the head, then peeked over and looked at me! I was stunned and felt so blessed to be able to see something like that.

When working with a young man in Virginia, I became aware of a small gold 'Puff' dragon that was quite playful. At one spot on the spine, I had placed a small gold Fluorite wand and as this magikal bit of energy encountered the wand, it squealed with joy then wound itself around and around it. I went on with the session and when I had moved the energy to the head area, I again became aware of 'Puff' who informed me it was about time I got there! He was delightful.

Another time a young woman had come to me to help her overcome a very abusive childhood. She had little fun in her life and we talked a bit about what she could do to create that. I told her about the dragons and she began to see the one associated with her. She asked if I would take a ride with her on the back of the dragon and as we soared through the air, imagination turned to magik that became real. We laughed with the thrill of it all. I know she has had many happy times doing this.

While working with one client, I became aware of a huge dragon that was moving very slowly and wasn't going to be hurried. I was attempting to energize him a little when he turned around and looked at me with solemn eyes and very distinctly said, "I will take care of this one!" That was surely okay with me!

I came to understand that the different colors of the dragons are influenced by the vibration of the color ray of the individual. In other words, as we raise our vibrations, the colors change as we work our way through the chakras. The colors are wondrous. A deep, velvety purple with glistening white trim, a warm, mahogany brown, a dark forest green, almost black and a sunshiny lemon yellow are some of the colors I've seen. I've also seen long eyelashes on the 'girls'. I understood from the Masters that the colors reflect where we are on our path and that they are associated with the guides and Masters working with us at any given time. The dragons manifest for me as living entities with distinct personalities. I very much enjoy playing with them.

Nothing is separate. The serpent has always been associated with wisdom and Eden. The reason it has been associated with evil is because of the egoic mind's fear that if I don't know what you are doing, you must be up to something. And that 'I don't see it, I don't see it,' is still like a battle cry of the logical mind. 'I don't see it. I don't get it, what are they doing there?' It is to relax, take a deep breath and feel it. The kundalini has always risen in the human being somewhere around the first opposition of the planet Uranus, so somewhere between the ages of 38 and 42. The kundalini rises, for many of the children of the stars, a lot earlier, in these times. As the kundalini rises, it makes the individual much more aware of how it feels to be powerful. It makes people aware of their power so a lot of them will stop the kundalini around the heart chakra. The kundalini in the lower three chakras very often stirs the sexual energy, not that that is what it's about because it is about power. But, since sexuality is one of the power issues of life, then as the sexuality is stirred and there is so much fear of it getting out of control, it is a little like Pandora's box. She was told not to open it but curiosity about what would happen if she did, brought about chaos. So, when the people allow the kundalini to come to the heart chakra and it reaches a point of balance, at least in the physical world, people can experience controllable religious fervor. As the kundalini rises on past the heart chakra, it comes to the thymus or thirteenth chakra. It lies in the area of the thyroid and the thymus. It actually activates a deeper wisdom of one's spiritual self but people are afraid of it. As religion has taught you what you have to do to be good, it has also suggested that if you allow yourself to discover your higher consciousness, the truth of your spiritual being, it endangers you. It isn't safe for people to know that and of course not, because the church wants to be in power and it doesn't want any human individual recognizing what is within themselves. I Am A Master. As the kundalini moves up into the throat chakra, it begins to really stir the considerations of the willingness to become one with the will of God. I Am That I Am. So many people question what that really means. What does 'I Am That I Am' mean to me? It means that as God Is, I Am. That is how God created. It does not mean that some human being is going to take over God's position because God is always moving and growing and changing, creating and manifesting. Humanity has been so fearful of the power, desperately wanting it, but wanting it to use as 'this is how I want to use it.' The ego mind just dreams of having all the money in the world. And yet, what the ego does not take into consideration is that there is no 'there.' Logic has attempted to present the concept of 'there' but 'there' would be tantamount to sitting on a cloud and playing a harp for eternity. Humans were not created to be in stasis. When someone gets the idea that they are 'there', if they don't set new goals and get moving, if they don't act, 'there' is stasis. The kundalini rises and brings a remembrance of the connection with the divine. When you remember your connection to the divine, you are put on notice so that you recognize there is no 'there.' There is always change. There is always something new and when people decide that they don't have to do anything, they don't have to change at all, dis-ease begins to set in. The kundalini is the inspiration of the life. It is the eternal remembrance of wisdom. It is the consistent recognition of 'I am a divine, creative master.' So, the kundalini is the sacred serpent and doesn't stir up the beingness.

# 12

# ASCENDED MASTERS

*"What if you slept and what if in your sleep you dreamed and what if in your dream you went to heaven and there you plucked a strange and beautiful flower, and what if when you awoke you had the flower in your hand? Oh, what then?"*

*- Samuel Taylor Coleridge*

**Who are the Ascended Masters?** Ascended Masters are those who have worked through lifetimes to experience and heal emotions. Emotions keep us in the cycle of reincarnation until we wake up and realize that once we work through the lessons we have chosen to experience, we can upward spiral our energy or ascend. It is a process and it can't be accomplished in a day, a month, a year or even in one lifetime. It is giving up everything that you think you can't live without in order to have it all. All of the greatest teachers the world has known have ascended in order to aid us from a space of extreme clarity and love without a condition. Other Masters have chosen to remain in the earth plane to teach those who are close to awakening and to experience the evolution of humanity. It isn't just the greatest teachers that have ascended. It might be those 'ordinary' people who have awakened to who they truly are—Divine Creative Masters. I value the help and guidance I've received on my journey. Just keep in mind that the Masters wait to be asked before they can begin to help you..

## FIRST RAY

El Morya is the master of the first ray of energy and his color is a deep electric blue. For those opening up to the energy of El Morya, they will often see deep electric blue spheres out of the corner of their eyes but when they turn to look, the spheres are not there. But, they really are. This master is wondrously loving. He, along with the master Serapis Bey, is considered a tough taskmaster but he is also the master that takes the initiate, the new soul-seekers on the first beginnings of their journey. El Morya is a master who works with the throat chakra and he will energetically bring the ability to speak the truth. He works closely with the master Hilarion. The energy of the old lessons has changed somewhat as humanity is rushing headlong into a whole new cycle of human evolution. So, the teachings are different and how the teachings are given is different and the masters' presentation with humanity is sometimes considered startling different. El Morya is a master of will. 'I will to will Thy will.' There is a necessity to surrender and a lot of people are having issues with the throat; everything from a sore throat, a dry throat, a hacking cough, those things that are associated with the resistance to surrendering will. El Morya brings the opportunity for people to understand how to surrender their will, how to go into the solar plexus chakra, the soul center, and as they connect with their soul's evolution, they also begin to feel that ability to tell the truth so much more easily. The patriarchy has thought nothing of telling what they have called 'white lies.' There is no consideration that if you are being dishonest with others, you are the first one to reap the outcome of the dishonesty. Whatever is created returns to the creator first. The willingness to surrender will to God is imperative. Release control, let it go and be willing to feel, not just think about or analyze, debate or argue but to feel the truth. That opens the way, heart and soul, into the solar plexus. 'Know the truth and the truth shall set you free.' El Morya's task, more in these times, is to start an initiate on their path, because the souls that are on the earth now are not new. These are not first-time people. There are no new souls. There are souls who have had more experiences in some other place, another planet, another galaxy, another universe. El Morya still assists those who are seeking blindly in these times, looking for something that they don't even know or are not even sure of what it is they are looking for. A stone representing this ray might be Azurite.

## SECOND RAY

Lord Lanto is the master of the second ray of energy. His color is a pale yellow. His task is the refinement of the solar plexus, the yellow ray. Lord Lanto and the master Kuthumi, these are the masters that really align with love without a condition. Unconditional love is not something that humanity has ever known in such a very long time because there are so many judgments, there are so many conditions. 'You can only love if it is this way or that way. You can only love certain people. You can only love if they are 'good.' And yet what is the definition of good? The patriarchy says that they are good if they agree with me and they are bad if they don't. That isn't a definition of goodness. It might be a definition of abandonment of personal power. It may be a situation of fear. 'I want to be on the 'right' side when things come down.' So, Lord Lanto assists the unconditional love, love without a condition, enlightened so that the heart is light. Lord Lanto has sought always to bring humanity to that place of the eternal knowledge of the love in such a measure that the judgments simply pass away. One stone associated with this yellow ray is the pale-yellow Citrine.

## THIRD RAY

Lord Paul, the Venetian, oversees this ray. This radiates a soft pink color. Lord Paul is an artisan master. He is a master teacher of beauty, of creativity and love without a condition. It is amazing how the masters will fall into a level of energy, but each one will bring different threads or different streams to the overall flow. In these times, the masters are seeking to bring to humanity a remembrance of unconditional love, how God loves, not recently, but truly how God has always loved. The ego mind has sought to present God as a patriarchal father, cruel and punishing and very proud. Lord Paul seeks to help humanity to remember that war heals nothing, so, love without a condition, the focus on beauty, the recognition of personal creative ability. All of that is so vitally necessary and more so in these times, perhaps more than it has ever been. His pink color is associated with the heart, the throat, and the solar plexus and the logical mind would say, "That isn't what I have learned." Humanity is being called to remember that there is so much more to you than you have ever known. There is so much more to you than you have been told. There is so much more than the logical mind believed it could deal with so the ego mind attempted to make things simple by limitation, by denial of elements that are so purely assistive. And yet, if they didn't support conflict, if they did not fit into the rules and regulations of religion, then the logical mind simply dismissed them, personal magik, the power of human creativity, divine creative masters. To this day, so many would be so horribly offended at the idea that a human could be divine and yet, you cannot ascend if you deny who you are. So, we are blessed with the energy of Lord Paul who is loving, gentle and strong.

## FOURTH RAY

Serapis Bey is master of this ray and he resonates to the color white. His primary teaching is discipline and the ego really doesn't want to discuss it, it doesn't want to think about it, and it doesn't want to hear about it. Discipline, in order to keep people away from it, actually moved into a place that the mind sees as militaristic, controlling, dominant, and yet, discipline is energetically about the ability to be with yourself so powerfully that you will not abandon yourself. In this process, a spiritual revolution is begun. Serapis Bey brings clarity of purpose and joy. The ego mind has done its best to convince humanity if you're going to live a spiritual life, then you get to give up fun, that a spiritual life is two-thirds more serious and it is that it is loaded with judgments, pomposity, rigidity and 'that's just how it is' and you do as you're told and you don't argue about it. So, the majority of humanity would not be heaven bound if they paid any attention to what the church says about what discipline brings. Serapis Bey, quite frequently, is the master who becomes the gatekeeper to those who are the most difficult, undisciplined, angry, war-like people. This gives him the reputation of being a very tough taskmaster because he takes tough love to bring wounded people home to themselves so that they can really feel what is required for their evolution. Serapis Bey is associated with the deep red Ruby.

## FIFTH RAY

The master Hilarion oversees this ray. He resonates to the color green and he is a truth teacher, he is a master of technology, he has understood throughout time how science and magik are very much a part of this thing. Hilarion has been called a tough taskmaster. He was Saul of Tarsus, Paul, in the bible. He was a short-tempered, impatient, judgmental man who did not have very much good to say about women, partly because he was a gay man. He has not been considered a master anyone would particularly like to deal with. And yet, all of the masters have, as time has passed, deepened the allowing of loving within themselves, moved into a compassion that could serve humanity rather than using brute force, war games and control. Hilarion is a master that is very much involved in the technology of the times and how that technology is changing where humanity is going now, spiritual evolution, the blending of science and spirit. So, there are a lot of changes you can see and feel. The Emerald is his crystal.

## SIXTH RAY

Lady Nada oversees this ray along with Jesus. Her purple is the royal purple. Jesus resonates to the royal purple and the rose-red. Their energies are about strength and nobility of spirit much more than some superior position because of who they are. Humanity has so many wounds because of all of the judgment and displacement. 'Who has the most money? Who has the most status? Who has the most power? Who is the best known? Who is the most beautiful?' Those are temporary, very temporal, quickly passing and yet, they have been held up as the standard for how the people would perform. So many people, talented people, brilliant people, people who are amazing beings, have disallowed themselves of truly allowing their light to shine because of judgments of status. Lady Nada is a very cool-headed business woman. She has a very keen mind and a very clear eye about the legalities of good business, the balance. She can balance the books. She understands the law, both human and divine and some would call her a no-nonsense woman. And yet, she is very compassionate because she doesn't allow herself to get caught up in conditions. She operates in the compassionate objectivity. "I see who you are, not who you believed when you doubted yourself or what the world has said by what they think they see." Any of the deep purple stones would represent this ray.

## SEVENTH RAY

St. Germain oversees the seventh ray and his color is violet. This master is stepping into the position of world teacher for the Aquarian Age which will actually give many of the totally religious an opportunity to get over the shock. Many of them will want to fight about the fact that he is trying to knock their Master from the throne. They become highly incensed he is trying to take the position of both world teacher and leader away from Jesus. It would be the last thing that St. Germain would consider, to dethrone the Other. Neither office has a throne. But, the energy of the Piscean Age is passing with the Piscean Age, as the teachings of the Aquarian Age are much more about quality, about unity, about oneness, things that humanity simply has not been willing to consider because it is not competitive. It is about things that have been forgotten in the inner world. That is where the Aquarian Age will take things. To be deeply connected within is also to be connected without. The more you connect within yourself, the more you have clarity about how you function in the world. As a master teacher of clarity, as a master of ceremonial magik, St. Germain brings the world a new perspective, at least it is new to the world now. It's so ancient that it is new again. Remember who you were in the beginning and you will very comfortably understand how St. Germain is the Divine Creative Master. Amethyst is usually associated with St. Germain and there are some of these crystals that are decidedly violet.

# REFLECTION

## EPILOGUE

*Choosing what you want to do, and when to do it, is an act of creation.*

**Many years have passed since my awakening and I keep on learning.** There have been times when I just wanted to stop and take a break. But what would I do then? The crystals and stones are so much a part of me that I couldn't live a full life without them. I remind myself from time to time that each of us is unique and we each have our own particular gift to share with others. Who would share the gift you have if not you? I feel so grateful that I discovered my passion when I did. I would not be where and who I am had I not embraced that.

The last few years have been full of upheaval in lots of ways. My partner and soul flame of thirty years passed on to work in spirit. He was always there for me and one of my most passionate supporters. My mother made her transition shortly thereafter. I found myself one day asking, "My life has turned upside down so what am I going to do about it? I know, I'll build a healing center!" And, I did. The last three years have been incredible. I have done so much soul-searching while creating my dream of a healing center that is a haven for those who are awakening and searching. I've begun to remember who I truly am and I'm happy and truly blessed. I'm teaching certification classes for crystal healers and keeping up with doing the layouts, and it's still my passion! Wait! Surely that isn't a nudge I feel??!

*"The truth of one's soul is silent, important only to oneself, for my truths are not necessarily your truths. So, silent it will be until in silence our truths will meet and we laugh to find that they are only reflections of one another."*

*- Nari*

# Linda Thomas

## ABOUT THE AUTHOR

Linda Thomas has lived most of her life in northern Wyoming. It is a wonderful place to live and there is also an abundance of rocks! Since early childhood, she has collected stones that seemed to call to her. Some weren't very pretty but she loved them all.

As the years passed, she began to feel a longing to explore a mystical, spiritual life. When the student is ready, the teacher appears. She had many teachers and experiences that led her along her chosen path. An important part of that path was the purchase of the local bookstore. Forgoing her job of eight years, she gained a world of experience and met incredible people. One of the things she added to the inventory was a variety of stones and crystals.

Her love affair with crystals began in the bookstore. She read everything she could find on the crystals and crystal healing which wasn't very much. She was thrilled when a friend told her about a crystal certification class that was beginning. She drove two hundred miles a week for three months in the middle of a Wyoming winter! Linda didn't know much about the crystals at that point but when the instructor demonstrated a layout on the body, she wanted to tell her to step aside, she knew how to do this! She received her certification in crystal healing in January of 1988 and never looked back.

Linda discovered early on that she worked with ascended masters. They guided her throughout her healing sessions and continue to do so. Through the process of laying stones on the body, an integration of the mental, emotional, spiritual and physical bodies is achieved.

Linda has traveled all over the country doing lectures, classes and healing sessions. And one thing has never changed-her love of the crystals. She looks forward to many more years spent in the energy of these crystalline beings! Visit her at www.eternal-ice.com